The 13th Day of Christmas

The Story of Mars 1

Robert Blevins

All Rights Reserved

The 13th Day of Christmas ©2011 by Robert Blevins
Edited by Geoff Nelder of Great Britain
First Edition in Paperback
Published by Adventure Books of Seattle
www.adventurebooksofseattle.com
'The Small Press from the Great Northwest'

ISBN 13: 978-0-9823271-5-9
Country of First Publication: U.S.A.
Cover art and interior book design
© 2011 by Adventure Books of Seattle

My sincere appreciation to the following people and organizations for their assistance and inspiration in the creating of this novel
Ray Bradbury
Neil Marr of BeWrite.net
The Jet Propulsion Laboratory in Pasadena, California, U.S.A.
The Mars Exploration Program at NASA/JPL
Julie Payette – Chief Astronaut, Canadian Space Agency
Neil Armstrong, Buzz Aldrin, and Michael Collins of Apollo 11

Image Credits

NASA Photojournal
The Jet Propulsion Laboratory
Adventure Books of Seattle Image Files

Table of Contents

Prologue

'Ad astra per aspera'
(A rough road leads to the stars)

A cold and miserable rain had been falling on Washington D.C. for a week, casting a damp and oppressive pall over the city. Ashen clouds rolled overhead in an endless parade, dumping their heavy loads of moisture like worshippers filing past a shrine to throw pennies at its feet. A sharp wind snapped through the streets, tormenting any pedestrians unlucky enough to be out in the weather. Water spilled from gutters and potholes filled. Sewers in several parts of the city had flooded, retreated, and then flooded again.

President-elect Graham Richardson watched the pounding rainstorm from the rear seat of the limousine as it splashed its way along the sodden streets. Richardson was dressed in a conservative blue suit with a gray tie. A driver and a single Secret Service agent rode up front.

The glass partition between the front and back seats rolled down with a soft hum.

A young black man in the front scooted around in his seat and spoke politely. "Mr. President?"

"Yes?"

"It just came over the radio, sir. The First Lady has arrived from Boston and is now addressing the crowd."

"She's stalling them until we arrive, Agent Davis. I think they enjoy Sarah's speeches more than my own."

"We're only two minutes away, Mr. President. She won't have to stall them very long."

"And we are late. My fault, I know."

"I'm sure everything will be fine, sir."

"My apologies for the delay." Richardson held up a large paper cup. "I've never liked hotel coffee. This is *real* coffee."

"Yes, sir."

"You've been a great help, Agent Davis. I appreciate it."

"You're welcome, Mr. President." The window hummed back into place.

Richardson was late to his own inauguration due to an unscheduled stop at a local coffee shop. After ordering the limo to pull over, he had walked boldly into the little bistro. To the extreme shock of the early-bird patrons, he had ordered a latte with skim milk, tipped the waitress five dollars, and then headed back to the limo. A crowd of well-wishers had quickly gathered around the car.

After Agent Davis allowed a discreet amount of glad-handing by his new boss, he gently reminded the President-elect of the time. The limousine and its entourage of motorcycle cops rolled away into the rainstorm and toward the Capitol building. That had been five minutes ago.

Richardson found the paper copy of his speech and opened it for a last quick look. *They will probably say it's too Kennedy, or too idealistic, or too something*, he thought. He tucked the paper back into his pocket.

The limo braked to a sudden halt. A dozen Secret Service agents flocked around the car and took their assigned positions. One of them opened the door.

Graham Richardson, the formerly obscure junior senator from Colorado, stepped from the car and waved to the roaring crowd.

They were a sea of umbrellas in the pouring rain, people with wet faces and smiles and cameras flashing without end. Richardson began a slow walk past the crowds; stepping to the restraining ropes occasionally to shake hands. He noticed the Secret Service agents were professionally scanning the spectators for possible trouble, but at that moment, Richardson was unafraid. He had a strange thought. *No one hates me today. I haven't had enough time to screw things up.* When he smiled at his little private joke, the crowd cheered even more. They thought he was smiling at them.

Richardson headed toward the stage and took out the paper

copy of his speech. The rain was already causing the ink to run across the paper. He folded it a couple of times and thrust it back into his pocket. He would just have to wing it. He saw his wife at the podium and at that same moment, she spotted him and stepped away from the microphone.

Sarah Richardson's expression was one of tearful pride and disbelief. The new First Lady waved at her husband and then clapped her hands, encouraging the crowd to do the same. They erupted with even more applause and cheers.

Richardson shook hands with the Vice President-elect, and then acknowledged the clamoring assemblage who stood waiting under a massive ocean of umbrellas. The rain continued to beat down on those umbrellas, but it had no effect on the fire of their exhilaration. The sound was like a thousand Zulu warriors pounding on their leather shields, celebrating the coming new era. They shouted his name and waved their arms, each trying desperately to elicit some response, or perhaps a bit of eye contact.

My God, he thought. *There are so many of them. It looks like Woodstock or something.*

Richardson was humbled, but he also felt a kinship with the crowd because he understood the reason for their excitement. He had won the election on a simple platform. He had promised to maintain his predecessor's policy of bringing change and hope to America. That man had served two popular terms and arguably saved the nation from a repeat of the Great Depression. He had accomplished many of his goals, while others were left undone. It was up to Richardson to finish this work, as well as moving forward with some ideas of his own. Richardson had made promises to the voters and now it was time to make good on those promises.

The Chief Justice approached him holding the old family Bible that Richardson had provided earlier for the swearing-in ceremony.

He placed his left hand on the Bible and held up his other hand. He had the will and the desire to succeed. He wondered if he had the strength. As he began reciting the Oath of Office, he hoped he did.

White House Meeting

H oward Tyler was slightly built, with thinning silver hair and eyes as blue as the ocean. He had been with NASA for sixteen years and its executive director for the last five. Even working with an ever-decreasing budget, he had boldly led NASA to a string of successes during his tenure. Probes, orbiters, and landers had visited several planets throughout the solar system. Nearly every known asteroid had now been catalogued and their orbits tracked for possible dangers to Earth. The International Space Station was three times its original size and operational.

A pleasant young woman with a slight Southern accent and a pretty smile touched him gently on the shoulder. "Sir, the President will see you now."

"Thank you." Tyler followed her into the Oval Office.

Graham Richardson stood up from behind the desk and extended his hand. "Thanks for coming today. Please have a seat."

Tyler felt the powerful grip as the President greeted him warmly. *He looks a lot taller in person.* "Thank you, Mr. President." He sat down on the other side of the table and laid the thick folder on his lap, like a weapon ready to do battle.

"I have a proposal for you, Dr. Tyler."

"I'll answer any questions I can, Mr. President." Tyler held up the folder. "I've also brought a copy of our latest budget numbers."

"Good. Can you can leave them with my secretary after we're finished?" Richardson looked away for a moment.

"Of course, Mr. President. Is there something wrong, sir?"

"No." Richardson pulled open a drawer and took out a small paperback book. He laid it on the desk. "Have you ever seen this?"

Tyler picked up the book and glanced at it. Splashed in bold letters across the front were the words *The Martian Chronicles*. "Uh, yes sir. I read it in high school. I like Ray Bradbury, but I don't understand your meaning."

"You will. I didn't ask you here to discuss budget numbers." Richardson's eyes twinkled as he spoke. "I'll bet you thought that's why I asked you here today, right?"

"To be honest, yes." Tyler said.

"Not even close," said Richardson. "Can you give me an update on the Mars Exploration Program?"

Tyler was taken aback by the unexpected question. "Well, Mr. President, currently we have four rovers on the Martian surface, three orbiters mapping the entire planet, and last year we brought back thirty-six pounds of rock and soil on that sample-return mission."

"Yes. That was certainly a miracle of engineering," said Richardson." Let me come right to the point, Dr. Tyler. How close are we to actually putting a man on Mars?"

Tyler had answered the when-are-we-going-to-Mars question more times than he could remember. He recited his usual response, almost by rote. "At present funding levels, we think we could launch a manned mission sometime between 2030 and 2040."

Richardson leaned across the desk and looked hard at Tyler. "What if funding was increased? Do we have the technology to do it sooner?"

"How much sooner, Mr. President?"

"Say within three or four years."

Tyler shook his head. "No disrespect sir, but what you ask may be impossible."

Richardson pressed the point. "No chance at all?"

"Well, it's likely beyond our capabilities right now. The reality is in the cost, Mr. President. We would need three times our current yearly funding to consider such a program, maybe more. I would have to check with our Mars Exploration Program supervisors at JPL. We have a few designs for a Mars vehicle system, but nothing concrete."

"Well, I suggest you start looking at those designs again."

"Sir?"

"I'm holding a press conference this afternoon, Dr. Tyler. I'm going to announce that I'm committing this nation to a manned mission to Mars."

Tyler's heart pounded against his ribs. He sat up straighter in his chair and listened sharply. The budget notes were forgotten.

"I want you to get together with your MEP people," said Richardson, "and create a feasibility study. I need the results of this study within ninety days."

"Feasibility study, sir?"

"Exactly. We're going to make a deal here, Dr. Tyler. If your people at MEP say we can do it, I will guarantee the funding and we will put people on Mars. However, there is one catch."

"Yes, sir?"

"We would have to launch this mission within forty-two months."

Tyler did a quick mental calculation. "Three and a half years? That's not much time for a program of this scale, Mr. President."

Richardson nodded. "I understand it's a tough request, but I may not win a second term, Dr. Tyler. The next President may not be so generous, and a Mars program could be the first thing on his chopping block agenda. Understand me, this is an all-or-nothing proposition."

Tyler managed to blurt out, "I'll do my best, sir."

"That's all I ask." Richardson turned in his chair and stared out the window. "You know, doing this could help improve our role as a world leader in science and technology. We're still behind the Japanese and a few other countries. This is not acceptable. My science advisors say a good launch window to Mars comes up in three years."

"Yes, sir. Actually, the window comes around about every two years. The one you are talking about is better than most."

"How long would it take for a manned mission to reach Mars, if we took advantage of this window?"

"That depends on the route, Mr. President. We normally use a longer, fuel-saving route when we send out probes. For a manned mission, well, we would want to get our people there and back as quickly as possible. Maybe four months each way on a manned mission, sir. Plus any time they remain on the surface. *And about as easy as climbing Mount Everest in tennis shoes,* he wanted to add.

"We have people on the International Space Station who have orbited the Earth for more than a year," Richardson said.

Tyler fidgeted in his seat, searching for the right words. "Well, meaning no disrespect Mr. President, but sending people to Mars is much more challenging than orbiting the Earth in the ISS."

"I'm sure it is, Dr. Tyler. I'm just asking your people to decide if it's possible, that's all. Tomorrow morning I'm going to ask Congress for six billion dollars in initial funding for what we're calling the Mars Project. I will be contacting officials from the Canadian Space Agency and asking for their support. You *must* put the CSA into the loop and make them active participants. We will need their help."

"Mr. President, when you say 'put them into the loop,' you mean what exactly?"

"One of the actual mission crew will have to be Canadian."

"Funding assistance, sir?"

"That's right. This needs to be a joint effort. If we include one of their own astronauts in the project, I can guarantee their full support."

"I understand, sir."

Richardson stood up and extended his hand again. "I have another meeting now, Dr. Tyler. Remember, I need a go or no-go from NASA within ninety days."

"You'll have it, sir." Tyler picked up his budget folder, shook the President's hand, and left the Oval Office. His feet barely touched the floor on the way out. He mumbled something to the President's secretary, dropped the budget file on her desk, and left in a daze.

As he headed down the hall, Tyler made a quick mental list of the people he would have to call later. It was a long list. In a few short moments, he had gone from being a budget administrator attempting to squeeze the maximum from every public dollar to facing the biggest challenge of his life. His mind raced with possibilities and scenarios. As his Secret Service escort led him through the White House and outside to his rental car, a smile spread across his face from ear to ear.

Tyler drove a few blocks away from the White House until he came to the first spot where street parking was allowed. Pulling the car over to the curb, he called a number on his cell phone.

"Assistant director's office," answered a female voice. "How may I help you?"

"Hello, Doris. This is Dr. Tyler. May I speak to Jim, please?"

There was a click on the other end of the line. "Morris here."

"Hi, Jim. How's your morning?"

"Busy as hell. How did it go with the President? Do we have to cut back on office supplies again?"

"No. And you're not going to believe what he wants us to do." Tyler explained the President's proposal, including the short amount of time they had to accomplish the task.

"He can't be serious," said Morris. "Does he have any clue how much money this will cost, and what is involved?"

"I think he knows the basics, Jim. Tomorrow he's asking Congress for six billion in new funding earmarked specifically for a manned mission. I'm flying down to JPL this afternoon. I'm calling an emergency meeting with the MEP team for ten a.m. tomorrow."

"We're going to need a helluva lot more than six billion," said Morris. "And why is he only giving us forty-two friggin' months?"

"He wants us to try it before the next election. I'll explain later.

We have to figure out a way to come through on this, I mean – if we can do it at all. If we screw the pooch on this one we'll be right back to tight budgets and mission cuts. It's a roll of the dice, and NASA's future is riding on it."

"As long as we don't crap out," said Morris sardonically. "I'm not sure we can even get past the planning stage in that short a time."

"Can you fly out to Pasadena tomorrow? I need you at that meeting," Tyler said. "The MEP team is the only ones who can say whether a mission in that timeframe is possible. The President wants a feasibility study on his desk in ninety days. That's not much time to work out the details."

"Are you kidding?" Morris said. "Of *course* I'll be there. I wouldn't miss it for the world."

By the time Howard Tyler's flight touched down in Los Angeles a few hours later, word of the President's decision had reached the press and spread across the country – and the world – like a prairie wildfire.

The cable news channels and blogs were already filling with voices either heralding the President's decision or ridiculing it as a waste of taxpayers' money.

Tyler plucked his bags from the luggage carousel and headed for the rental car counter. As he worked his way through the airport crowds, he spotted a newspaper kiosk. One particular headline leaped out in bold lettering:

RICHARDSON COMMITS U.S. TO MARS MISSION

Tyler stopped just long enough to buy a copy.

The Tuna Can

When Howard Tyler entered the meeting room at the Jet Propulsion Laboratory in Pasadena, the buzz of voices ceased. Fifty scientists and administrators from the Mars Exploration Program were waiting impatiently for him; most were sitting at tables scattered around the room. All eyes fell on Tyler as he went to the front. "All right, quiet down," he said. "I'm sure you've heard the news by now. Our new President wants us to go to Mars."

The room burst with applause and cheering.

Before Tyler could say more, the door swung open again and a tall man with short blond hair and a huge smile waved to everyone. He was dressed in the standard NASA coveralls normally reserved for astronauts. A hastily drawn Mars 'mission patch' made of cardboard was pinned to the front of his suit. The big man with a sense of humor was Jim Morris.

"Hey! Anyone here like this?" Morris shouted, tapping the 'mission patch.'

More cheers erupted from everyone; a few people laughed.

Morris took a seat on the corner of a table near the front of the room.

Tyler gave him a firm thumbs-up and then faced the MEP team. "The President has handed us a job, folks. You've heard the good news. Now comes the bad. He's only giving us three and a half years to get it off the ground."

It was as if someone had pulled the plug on the stereo at a party. The happy celebration was replaced by stunned silence.

"Impossible!" someone shouted. Loud protests shot around the room with several of the MEP team trying to make their points. A few seconds later, the roar of confusing voices made it difficult to understand anything.

"Quiet down! Listen up!" Tyler yelled above the noise. The raucous disorder settled to a low grumbling. "I know this is a shock, but before we go any further, understand something. The President is giving us a shot at Mars. Congress has authorized six billion in initial funding. Those are the facts. I'm not saying it will be easy, but anyone who wants to throw in the towel can walk out the door right now. Effective immediately, all upcoming Mars missions not related to the Mars 1 project are officially on hold. That means probes, rovers, orbiters slated for launch, everything. I'm freezing those missions right now. All available resources are now committed to Mars 1, until we decide whether or not we can do it."

Ken Coltrin, head of the manned-space flight division for the Jet Propulsion Laboratory, rose from his seat. "There's only one realistic way to go to Mars in such a short time, Dr. Tyler."

"How's that?"

"We've known for years *how* to do it." Coltrin flipped up his fingers one at a time as he made his points. "First, you have to design and build a habitat for the crew and put it on the Martian surface. Second, you need a crew vehicle to get the astronauts there and back. Third, you need a landing-and-return vehicle that will deliver the crew safely to the Martian surface and back up to the crew vehicle for the trip home. Then, you need a capsule to get them down from Earth orbit." Coltrin looked apologetic. "The problem is – we don't *have* any of these things."

"I know that," said Tyler. "Tell me what we *do* have."

Coltrin waved a hand in dismissal. "Not much. We have mission plans based on all the data we've collected since the Viking landers. The entire planet has been thoroughly mapped in high resolution. And we're training astronauts in Mars-like environments at Mono Lake and the Houghton crater in Canada. However, we just don't have the hardware. No one anticipated we'd be launching a manned mission to Mars for at least another ten years."

"Any vehicles in the works, even in the planning stages?"

Coltrin shook his head. "Just proposals on paper."

"So what can we do?"

"We have to review the available mission plans, select one of them, and then have the vehicles that fit that mission plan built quickly," Coltrin said. "But the safety margin for any crew on a rush program like this is going to drop, and I mean dramatically. At best, I would give such a mission only a fifty-fifty chance of success." He sat down. An uncomfortable silence dragged on for a few moments. Coltrin had summed up everyone's feelings about the situation precisely.

Tyler looked over at Morris. "What do you think, Jim? Can it be done, or not?"

Morris nodded vigorously. "I'm certain it can, but I'm in the minority. All the science teams have been buzzing since the President went public with this. Most of them believe it can't be done in three or four years. They're talking at least seven, maybe ten years. I do have some good news, though."

"Let's hear it."

"I took the liberty of briefing Richard Albertson at Marietta about the President's request. He put his best team together and they worked on it all night. Albertson sent me a message saying they can deliver a crew vehicle and a lander in twenty-eight months – if they have full funding."

"You mean unlimited funding," said Tyler.

Morris nodded. "More or less."

"What about a surface habitat for the crew?"

Morris shook his head. "Not a chance. That would take four to five years, minimum. Any mission plan will have to include the astronauts calling their lander home while they are on the surface."

Coltrin, upon hearing this statement, brushed it off at once. "Come on, Jim! Albertson would swear his grandmother was pregnant with twins if he thought it would land Marietta the contract on this. He could be blowing smoke. How can he be sure they can build these vehicles in such a short time?"

Morris was firm. "I sent him some vehicle concepts from the MEP files. His A-team reviewed them. They insist they can do it in time, but it's going to cost a lot of money."

"How much?" asked Tyler.

"At least five billion for the crew vehicle. Another three billion or so for the lander. It could go higher, and they want a big bonus for delivering them within twenty-four months."

Tyler passed a hand over his eyes tiredly. "Over ten billion dollars for two vehicles?"

"I'd say it may end up closer to fifteen billion. You *know* there will be cost overruns. If it doesn't go much higher than that, it's a bargain, believe me. From start to finish, I estimate the mission would cost about thirty billion dollars."

Tyler nodded. "Okay. Well, that's almost twice our yearly budget. What do you think, Ken?"

Coltrin stared at the floor. "I'd call it a pocketful of 'ifs'. *If* we can get some suitable vehicles on the launch pad in time, and *if* nothing goes wrong." He turned and addressed the entire room. "This isn't a four-day trip to the moon, gentlemen. It means up to five months for our people in transit each way, plus any additional time on the Martian surface. It's the biggest challenge NASA has ever faced."

"Are you saying it's a no-go?" Tyler asked.

"Not necessarily. However, you're talking about moving human beings through space a few hundred million miles and then keeping them alive for months in a hostile environment. We haven't sent anyone beyond Earth orbit since 1972. It presents problems. And if we can't even put a habitat on the Martian surface for the crew, how will they survive? During Apollo, they used the LEM as living quarters and measured the time they had on the moon in hours or days, not months. Seems hardly worth the effort to go to Mars if we can only stay a day or two."

"We'll work on that," said Tyler.

In the very back of the room, a thin young man with dark hair and glasses raised his hand. "Dr. Tyler?"

"Yes. You have something to add?"

"I may have an idea."

Tyler sensed instinctively that the young man in black slacks and old tennis shoes was serious. "Who are you?"

"Andy Collins, sir."

"You're part of that new research group from Cal Tech?"

"That's right, sir. We started looking at all the available mission plans as soon as the story broke in the press. Our group believes we have one that will work."

"We're listening."

The young man stood up and referred to a small notebook for a moment, flipping a few of the pages. "Well, all the current Mars mission plans call for multiple launches into low Earth orbit, plus having to develop several new spacecraft. It's a tall order, sir."

"We know. So what's your idea?"

"Dr. Coltrin is right. Forget the habitat. The only possible way to get to Mars in such a short time is by launching an Apollo-type mission, fully self-contained. One crew vehicle, one two-stage Mars lander, and an Earth return capsule, all in a single package."

"We've thought of that already," said Tyler. "It always comes back to the fuel. We cannot carry enough fuel to reach Mars and return, using only one combination vehicle. The payload would be massive. We'd need a heavy-lift rocket twice the size of the old Saturn five they used on Apollo, just to get the whole package off the ground."

"Right," said Collins, "the fuel is a key factor. Nevertheless, there is a way." He began speaking with more confidence. "We could downsize the flight crew from six to three. This will cut consumables use in half. We already have a working design for a Mars lander

20

using fuel-efficient RL-10 engines. We use four RL-10's for the descent stage, and two on the ascent stage. We could reduce the width of the crew vehicle from eleven to seven meters. This would cut our total payload by at least a third."

"The tuna can," someone said, chuckling.

Collins ignored the remark and continued reading from his notebook. "We could launch this smaller combination into Earth orbit using rockets we have now, perhaps the Magnum, or a Centaur. We send up the lander and attach it to the forward section of the crew vehicle. Then we ferry up six solid-fuel boosters and attach them to the Magnum, with the crew vehicle, the Earth Return Capsule, and the lander as the main payload up front. We use three of these attached SRB's to put the craft on a trajectory to Mars, leaving three for the return. For mid-course corrections, we use the Magnum rocket. When the crew comes home, they transfer over to the Earth return capsule and we bring them down. That's it."

"I've seen versions of that mission plan," said Jim Morris. "It involves aerobraking, correct?"

"Yes, sir. Aerobraking with heat shrouds would be necessary to achieve Mars capture, and we would have to use the same technique on the Earth return. Otherwise, too much fuel will be required."

No one objected outright to Collins' suggestions. 'Aerobraking' did solve many fuel problems. Everyone also knew it was dangerous, and had never been tried on a manned spacecraft.

Ken Coltrin shook his head and squinted hard at the young scientist. "Dr. Collins. You still haven't answered how you would supply a crew on the Martian surface. You can't do it with a single vehicle, even using a three-man crew. And what about fuel for the liftoff from Mars? None of those RL-10 designs can carry enough fuel to land on Mars and make it back into orbit."

Collins flipped through his notebook once again until he located a certain entry. "Actually, sir...that's not exactly true. Since this lander would be modified for three people instead of six, it *could* carry enough fuel to land and make Mars orbit again, with a small safety margin. For re-supply, we could send an unmanned cargo module to Mars first. This module would contain spare fuel for the

Mars lander and supplies for the crew, including a portable shelter we can attach directly to the Mars lander to give the crew a little more living space. We can limit this cargo module to twenty metric tons of payload and put it on the surface near their landing site."

"And if the module failed somehow? The whole mission would be a scrub," said Coltrin.

Collins shook his head. "Even without the module, the crew could still remain on the surface for about ten days. We call this the Short Mission scenario. The MEV lander design is substantially larger than an old Apollo LEM. It would be a little cramped, but survivable. If we can land the cargo module on the surface safely, they can stay on Mars up to four months."

"That's a big physical and psychological load," said Coltrin, "trying a long mission like that with only three people."

"Yes, sir. It is. We would need the best astronauts available."

"No kidding."

"I like it," said Morris. "You're sure we could keep our people on the surface for ten days, even without the use of the cargo module?"

"Yes, sir." Collins answered. "I'll admit it's a risk, but I think it's the only way to get the job done in the short amount of time we have."

"Sounds interesting," said Tyler. He stood up and looked around the room. "All right. I want all science teams to put their heads together. We have ninety days to submit a mission plan to the White House. Let's get to work."

As everyone packed up their laptops and paper notebooks, Ken Coltrin made a mental note to check Andy Collins' credentials and perhaps offer him a job over in Manned Flight.

The kid was smart as hell.

Sulphur, Nevada

S crambling on all fours over the loose rock, a young woman with short brunette hair and a determined expression struggled toward the summit of the hill. She was deeply tanned and in excellent physical condition. Perspiration poured into her eyes, burning with a salty sting she quickly brushed away. Cuts crisscrossed the palms of her hands and the white coveralls she wore were streaked with dirt. A mission patch on the front of the coveralls identified her as a NASA astronaut, and a second, smaller patch on her left shoulder bore the logo of the Canadian Space Agency.

A white-hot sun had heated the desert floor to a hundred and thirty degrees, making it impossible to continue walking out in the open. She was intent on finding shelter on the hill.

Anna Johnson made good progress up the slope. She finally scrambled over the top and sat down to rest for a few moments, breathing heavily. *Nothing like this back at Moose Jaw*, she thought. She took out a small pair of binoculars and scanned the surrounding area. She spotted a group of warehouses sitting at the foot of a long ridge several kilometers to the south. A chain-link fence surrounded the old buildings. Deep terraced steps slashed lengthwise along the side of the ridge, the leftovers from decades of strip mining.

She dropped her pack to the ground and pulled out her one remaining water bottle. She drank deeply, but it tasted flat and did little to alleviate her thirst.

The sun beat down on her with an awesome power. It was a constant weight punishing her for having the audacity to cross the Nevada desert in midsummer. The sun was an enemy that could not be subdued, only outwitted.

Johnson started gathering all the loose rocks she could find into a pile. Her hands were already blistered, but she ignored the pain. She kicked out every loose stone available and threw them into the growing pile.

After twenty minutes of rock gathering, she knelt down and went to work.

Build a good base first, she reminded herself. She stacked the rocks as if she were building a fireplace, creating a 'U' shape. She extended the arms of the 'U' out about a meter and a half on each side, until the structure resembled an open coffin. When the wall was about a half-meter tall all around, she rummaged in her backpack and located a small package wrapped in plastic and tore it open.

Johnson laid the Mylar sheet carefully across the top of the U-shaped wall, letting it drape over the stones. She weighed it down on top with a few smaller rocks, then shoved her pack through the opening at the bottom and crawled inside.

She felt the difference at once. The Mylar sheet reflected the sun away and it was much cooler inside the rock shelter. She found her water bottle and took a small drink.

As the heat finally grew tolerable, she took out her map and studied it. Johnson noticed how difficult the terrain had been between the start of her journey and the destination. When she compared it with the routes her companions had taken, she made a wry face. Her assigned route was several kilometers longer and over tougher ground. *No surprise there,* she thought. *I always get the short end of the stick on this crew.*

She set the alarm function on her watch to wake her just after sundown and laid down to rest. A few moments later, she was asleep.

Twenty-five kilometers east of the hill where Anna napped peacefully under her Mylar, a tall man dressed in white coveralls and a baseball cap sat in the shade of a large boulder. He was studying his own map and sipping from a water bottle. He took a small compass from his pocket and flipped it open.

Dale McKendrick lifted his eyes from the wrinkled paper and squinted against the sun, looking toward a long ridge on the horizon. *There it is*, he thought.

Sulphur, Nevada was a ghost town in a remote part of the state, about fifty miles northeast of Reno. It stunk of old chemicals and strip mines long abandoned. The awful smell wafted across the desert and assaulted his nostrils like a boxer delivering a good left hook.

The training exercise involved dropping off the astronauts at three different locations, then having them hike across the desert to rendezvous in the center of a rough triangle.

That center was Sulphur, Nevada.

McKendrick considered trying to cross the valley before dark. He thought about the food and water waiting in one of the abandoned buildings at the old site. *I wonder if Johnson and Walker are already there*. After glancing at the map again, he was sure Johnson would be the last to arrive. She had a lot farther to hike, thanks to Commander Walker's route assignments.

The sun was dipping over the horizon and painting the mountains in hues of blue and gold. The oven-baked air was dissipating at last, as a soft breeze washed across the landscape.

I'm getting too old for this crap, McKendrick thought. He folded up the map, and laid his head on his backpack. He would finish the hike in the cool of the evening.

Michael Walker plodded across the stark landscape like a robot, stopping occasionally to wipe his face with a handkerchief. He was on an old dirt trail that rolled up and down the low hills like a roller coaster. Sharp rocks lay scattered along the trail. The unrelenting summer sun seemed to focus all its power on him, turning the desert into a Dutch oven from hell.

He passed another shallow lakebed on the side of the road, dry since the last Ice Age. Deep cracks ran across its surface and tough clumps of sagebrush dotted the edge. A hard, dry wind sucked the moisture from his body with quiet efficiency. It was as if the wind had signed an agreement with the sun to beat him into the ground.

Walker stopped in the road and dropped his pack. He dug out a large bottle of water and took a deep drink. The ghost town was still fifteen kilometers ahead, perhaps another three hours' walk. He was determined to make it to the supply cache before the others.

Everyone had been required to add a bit of salt to his or her water supplies before the start of the exercise. This was standard practice for desert hikes. However, Anna Johnson had received just a little more salt in her water ration.

I'll bet she's activated her retrieval alarm already, he thought. He smiled through cracked lips and gasped at the pain. Nevertheless, his smile grew wider as he thought about Johnson becoming thirstier as she drank more of the over-salted water. He wasn't worried about her actually dying of thirst. She could always call for help. In his mind, he was already considering who would replace her on the prime crew. All of the astronauts on his alternate list were men, of course.

I told them she was a bad choice, he thought ruefully. *We don't need a woman tagging along on this mission. We need a third man.* He felt no guilt about his actions. He wiped a few drops of blood from his lips and kept walking.

Anna Johnson awoke to the beep-beep of her alarm watch and sat up inside her rock shelter. Her throat burned even worse now than when she had laid down to rest. She found her water bottle and took a small drink. She made a wry face. *Sure tastes bad.* The water barely satisfied her raging thirst.

In her backpack, she carried a small radio that sent out an emergency signal. Pressing a button on it would bring cool water and a helicopter in less than thirty minutes. She dug the radio from her bag and weighed it in her hand.

Johnson took another sip from the water bottle and finally realized what was wrong.

It was full of salt.

Walker, she thought. *It must have been Walker.*

She stuffed the radio into her pack and crawled from the shelter. The sun was already dipping below the horizon and the air was beginning to cool. Johnson grabbed her pack and headed back down the hill. She picked out the offending water bottle from her pack and tossed it into the brush without another thought.

She shouldered her backpack and started walking across the flats. A look of determination – *and anger* – flashed in her eyes.

A Mind of its Own

T hirty-six months had now passed since Tyler's meeting with the President. NASA and the Canadian Space Agency had embraced Andy Collins' Apollo-style mission plan with enthusiasm. What had seemed unattainable three years ago was quickly becoming reality. The Mars Cargo Module was already on its way to the Red Planet, via a roundabout, fuel-saving route and would arrive just ahead of the astronauts.

Upon reaching Mars, the module would plow head-on into the upper edges of the thin atmosphere and whiplash around the planet in a fiery aerobraking maneuver, before settling into a stable orbit. On command from Houston, it would then descend to the surface using a system of parachutes and braking rockets to touch down at the astronauts' planned landing site.

Assuming Walker, Johnson, and McKendrick made a safe landing in their Mars Entry Vehicle, they would then use a small rover to locate the module, lower its wheels to the ground, and tow it back to the MEV.

After organizing their supplies and topping up the fuel in the lander, they would begin daily treks for research and sample collection. At the end of four months, the three astronauts would climb into the upper stage of the MEV, and using the lower stage as a platform, blast off from the Martian surface to rendezvous with the orbiting crew vehicle. After transferring several hundred pounds of priceless rock and soil samples to the main crew vehicle, they would jettison the lander and head for home.

The mission plan was set for Mars 1.

The scientists at JPL and NASA continually discussed one factor that would determine success or failure: Fuel.

Fuel was certainly a commodity beyond price on the mission. To save fuel and cut payload as Andy Collins had first suggested, the crew vehicle or 'Transhab,' was now only seven meters wide, about half the size originally conceived by NASA engineers. It was nicknamed the 'tuna can,' because of its shape. It contained sleeping quarters, a central communal kitchen, exercise equipment, a treadmill, a tiny bathroom and shower, and a large plasma video screen for occasional pre-recorded entertainment. There was even a computer with Internet access (time-delayed), for the crew to check e-mails and fan messages from home. The Transhab would be the astronauts' home during their voyage to Mars and back.

Six solid-fuel SRB rockets had been 'strapped' around the outside of the main engine. They were similar to the boosters used on space shuttles, only smaller. Three of these disposable rockets would 'inject' the spacecraft toward Mars, and the other three would be used to break out of Mars orbit for the return to Earth. The margin for error with the fuel supply on the *Abraham Lincoln* was very small, and everyone hoped that any in-flight corrections would be minimal.

This assembly now waited for the crew in Earth orbit. Two astronauts were already on board the *Abraham Lincoln*, running systems checks and conducting different experiments. Their job would end when Walker, Johnson, and McKendrick arrived.

The Mars 1 crew was due to rendezvous with the *Abraham Lincoln* for the crew transfer in only sixteen more days.

Howard Tyler was surprised to find Jim Morris waiting outside his office when he came to work. "I thought you were still in Houston."

Morris opened the office door for the director. "We have a problem," he said.

"Another one?" Tyler said. "Come on in." Tyler dropped his briefcase near his desk and sat down. The pressure on him and everyone else involved in the Mars Project had been enormous, especially in the last six months. Setbacks large and small had plagued the hurry-up program, and finding solutions for many of them had been difficult. "Okay," he said tiredly, "I know you were in Houston last night, and today you're here. I assume this means bad news."

"It's the cargo module," said Morris. "We've been running system checks and discovered a glitch in the programming."

"What type of 'glitch'?"

"The guidance system refuses to accept our landing site commands. The damn thing wants to pick its *own* site. In fact, it's no longer responding to any commands at all."

"You're saying it now has a mind of its own. How the hell can it do that?"

Morris sat down. "The computer is programmed to make course adjustments during Mars entry if it detects anything that makes the prime landing site impossible. Small craters, boulders, canyons, things like that. The software is glitched. It won't accept our numbers for the landing site, even though we know it's good. We're trying to upload some new commands, but so far the computer isn't accepting them."

Tyler went over to a side table and poured himself a cup of coffee. "We should name the damn thing Hal," he said angrily. "Is there a backup for this problem?"

"Nothing we can do from here. Looks like any fix would have to come from the astronauts once they arrive in Mars orbit. JPL has run up some new software that should correct the problem. We can have the crew rendezvous in Mars orbit with the module, go EVA and load in the new software."

"Can they realistically do this?"

Morris looked doubtful. "Difficult at best. Some of the guys at MEP think the module will start Mars entry as soon as it finishes the aerobraking maneuver. Since our people are going to be ten days behind, if the module goes for an immediate landing, the crew will arrive too late to replace the software." He laid a folder on Tyler's desk. "It's all in the report from JPL. There are some options suggested."

Tyler opened the folder and glanced at it. "How many people know about this situation?"

"Practically everyone who matters."

"I want to see the crew immediately," said Morris, "before this breaks out in the press. Can you have them in my office this afternoon?"

"They can be here by tomorrow. They're on a desert exercise in Nevada. We can bring them here directly from Nellis."

"Do it. By the way, how's the situation between Walker and Johnson?"

"Not good," said Morris. "Walker's still asking about dropping her from the prime crew. There's even been some press about it, but we're playing it down as normal competition during training."

"How is she handling it?"

"She's handling it fine, trust me."

Tyler thought for a moment. "We could still replace Johnson with her backup. What do you think?"

"She's the best natural pilot I've ever seen. The more Walker adds to her training schedule, the more she excels. I say we stay the course with her. She knows how to handle Walker."

"Good. Have them in my office by tomorrow afternoon. I want to brief them personally on this, before they see it in the papers. And make sure you talk to Walker."

"I'll tell him." Morris headed for the door. "I don't think it will do any good, though. He keeps saying she can't cut it."

"What do you think?"

"She'll be fine. She's had some problems in the MEV simulator, but her last three runs were perfect."

"Then tell Walker to ease up on her unless he has a better reason than the fact she happens to be a woman. That launch date is right around the corner and this last-minute discord isn't good for the mission. These astronauts are already under tremendous pressure as it is. I'm not replacing her now."

After Jim Morris left the office, Tyler passed a hand across his eyes and picked up the cargo module report from JPL. *Nothing but one goddamn crisis after another,* he thought. He was nearly at his wit's end and the mission had not even launched yet. From the assembly workers on the line at Boeing and Marietta to the scientists and engineers from Cal Tech who had created the actual mission plan, thousands of people had worked double duty for three long years. Everyone was very excited about Mars 1 – and very tired.

Tyler scanned the report. He felt besieged as he read the different solutions to the cargo module problem suggested by the MEP team. All of them sounded risky, as usual.

Anna Johnson

J ohnson kept a steady pace as she hiked across the barren Nevada desert. The full moon cast an eerie cream-colored light on the dunes and sagebrush. Her throat burned with a terrible thirst and she thought again about the retrieval radio weighing heavily in the front pocket of her jumpsuit. Pushing a button on it would bring an Air Force helicopter and the water she desperately needed. However, it also meant admitting failure and allowing Commander Walker to win the game he had forced upon her.

The hell with him, she thought. Anna checked her compass and continued walking. Her legs ached and she had stopped perspiring – a bad sign that meant dehydration.

The ridge was visible in the distance and getting closer. She could already see the lights from the open warehouse where NASA had left the supplies and a vehicle for the drive back to Nellis Air Force Base and an upcoming three-day leave from training. Her spirits began to lift.

An hour later, she found the dirt track she had been seeking, a dusty little road leading into the ghost town. *Three more kilometers to go.* In the bright moonlight, she could see long gashes cut into the side of a mountain in the distance. Heavy machines and miners intent on stripping the mountain of minerals had once worked the ridges.

Black drainage hoses ran snakelike from the top of the ridges until they reached the valley floor. The bitter smell of sulphur was overpowering.

Anna passed a holding pond secured behind a chain-link fence with a skull-and-crossbones sign attached. *Danger! Cyanide!* It read. She knew the cyanide was a leftover from the mining process. Another sign, painted sloppily in red paint on an old piece of wood said, *Welcome to the Hellhole.*

No surprise they finally closed it down, she thought. She wondered how her father had ever worked at the place.

Sulphur had been designated a Superfund cleanup site twenty years back, but when the money ran out, so did the cleanup effort. The mine was little known and far from civilization. The closest human habitation was in Gerlach, a roadside stop about fifty miles to the south.

Anna pushed the main gate open and entered the operations area. A few white frame houses sat at the foot of the ridge. They were in surprisingly good shape considering they were over fifty years old. A couple of warehouses with rusted tin roofs sat near the old houses. She saw a few slivers of light peeking through the roof on one particular warehouse and headed for it.

The last hundred meters felt like a thousand to her tired feet and exhausted body. She finally reached the warehouse and went inside.

The old building was nothing more than a dirt floor with four corrugated metal walls and a high roof once used to store mining equipment. She glanced around and tried to make a shout, but her sandpaper-dry throat only produced a feeble croak. In the center of the dirt floor sat a brand-new Jeep Cherokee, white and polished, with a NASA logo on the door.

Anna realized she was the first to arrive and raised a fist in triumph. She popped the hatchback on the Cherokee. There were two cases of bottled water and a half-dozen military MRE ration packs, all neatly packed into a pair of cardboard boxes.

She reached for a water bottle and drained it in a few desperate gulps, then opened another. Grabbing one of the ration packs and a third bottle of water, she shut the hatchback and climbed into the front passenger seat of the Jeep.

The key was in the ignition. She turned it to the accessory position, and then switched on the two-way radio mounted in the dashboard. She pressed a button on the microphone. "Staging One, this is Johnson, do you read?"

"Andy Collins here, Anna. We read you. What's your situation?"

"Well, I made it. Walker and McKendrick are still out there somewhere. Either of them call in the choppers, yet?"

"That's a negative, Anna. Looks like everyone is going to finish the exercise. Good job and congratulations on getting there first. How do you feel?"

"Thirsty, Andy. By the way, where is everybody? I thought there was supposed to be a debriefing crew here along with the flight surgeon. There's no one around, just the Jeep and the rations."

"The briefing's been cancelled. New orders. All of you are to return to Nellis. Dr. Tyler wants to see you right away down at Cape."

"Did he say why?"

"Something about a glitch with the cargo module. I don't have the details."

Johnson took another drink. "I hope it's not too serious. We *need* that module, you know."

"I know. Dr. Tyler and Jim Morris will brief you tomorrow afternoon when you arrive. A jet is already standing by at Nellis to take you all back to Cape."

"Do you have a position on Mike and Dale?" she asked.

"According to his personal locator signal, Dale is less than three kilometers away, and Mike should be arriving in about fifteen minutes."

"Understood. Thanks."

"No problem, Anna. Have a nice trip."

"Roger that." Johnson switched off the radio. She thought about the salt in her water ration and the old anger rose to the surface. *We're getting closer to the launch every day and Walker's still playing games,* she thought.

Reclining in the soft leather seat made her feel a bit better. *Well, there goes the three-day pass,* she thought. *Again.* She leaned her head against the window and tried to relax. She closed her eyes and dropped off to sleep in seconds.

Anna Christine Johnson had come into the world during the biggest snowstorm to hit Quebec in twenty years. She was home-birthed in a spare bedroom, not by choice, but because the road to the hospital was buried in drifts two meters high. The tiny dark-haired girl emerged from her mother's womb with an angry scream and an attitude. The screaming eventually stopped, the attitude always remained.

Her parents knew early on that little Anna was special. Once she learned to talk, she became a nonstop question machine who barraged people about everything she saw in her young world. Living with the curious girl was like being a contestant on a twenty-four hour a day quiz show. After she learned to read, a large amount of the family's income was diverted to children's books.

When Anna was seven years old, her father lost his job teaching geology at a local junior college. The family's savings evaporated within a few months.

Her father finally found work in an unlikely place. An offer arrived from a large mining company in the United States. The mining company offered him a supervisory position at three times his previous wage. The family sold their old home and moved to a small, but comfortable house in the town of Gerlach, Nevada.

Gerlach consisted of eleven houses and a gas station. The only reason for the gas station was that Gerlach was the last stop before one of the most remote areas in Nevada. A single dirt and gravel road led out of town and up to a huge strip-mining operation. On maps, the mine was named Sulphur, as if it were an actual town. It consisted of nothing more than a half-dozen equipment warehouses and a few company-built homes.

After passing by the mine, the desert road eventually ended on a two-lane highway leading up to eastern Oregon. A sign out front of the filling station in Gerlach proclaimed LAST GAS FOR 100 MILES! The station did just enough business to operate at a profit, so it remained.

It was the only gas station that included items such as rifle ammunition, camping supplies, and towing chains. The locals made a trip into Fernley about once a week to do their real shopping. However, for tourists preparing to cross a hundred miles of rocky desert road in their RV's and campers, the old gas station was a necessary stop. Some of the townies made a few bucks on the side pulling stranded campers out of the desert. The rough roads were hard and unforgiving.

When the mine at Sulphur finally turned into an ecological nightmare, it was designated an EPA Superfund site and closed for cleanup. Paul Johnson lost his job. The family returned to Canada and settled down in Moose Jaw, Saskatchewan. Anna, now thirteen, thought she would never see Gerlach again, and she was happy enough with that idea.

For the first time she had something to do after school other than four-wheeling and target shooting with the boys in Gerlach. She joined all the science clubs at her new school and discovered a fascination for the sky.

Gerlach remained a stubborn outpost on the edge of a great desert. It remained abandoned, and the government never got around to finishing the cleanup.

Anna excelled in her studies, graduated high school early, and entered college when she turned sixteen. Only seven years later, she had earned degrees from both the University of Toronto and McGill University in Montreal. She got a Master of Applied Science at Toronto and an electrical engineering degree from McGill. She accepted a systems engineer position with IBM Canada.

For the next five years, Anna Johnson either lectured at or

attended six other universities. She worked for a year in Zurich as a visiting scientist for the IBM Research Laboratory. Later, she worked in robotics and human-machine interaction research. She received a dozen prestigious awards along the way, and learned to converse in Russian, French, English, Italian, and Spanish.

However, at age twenty-seven she realized she had reached a peak in her life. She could teach, or perhaps do research for any number of high-profile companies. It was likely she would receive a lifetime of awards over a long career.

She wanted more.

Anna applied to the Canadian Space Agency that summer for astronaut training. She was selected from a pool of six thousand applicants to become one of four new Canadian astronauts.

After a period of basic training, the CSA assigned her to work in robotics. To prepare for her first actual mission, she obtained her captaincy on a CT-114 military jet at the Canadian Air Force Base in her home town of Moose Jaw. She logged over 900 hours of flying time, including 500 hours on high-performance jet aircraft.

She was certified as a one-atmosphere, deep-sea diving suit operator, which was a common training program for Canadian astronauts. Working in a deep-sea suit was similar in many ways to working in space.

After eighteen months of additional training at NASA's Johnson Space Center in Houston, she made her first flight as a member of a shuttle crew. Her job was to assist in the deployment of a new space telescope. A year later, she was back in space on another shuttle mission. This time she helped transfer needed equipment and supplies to the International Space Station. Then the Space Shuttle program began winding down.

Three years passed and there were no more call-ups from NASA. The Space Shuttle had been replaced by the newer Crew Exploration Vehicle and the last existing shuttle was put into mothballs. It seemed as if Johnson's 'shot in the sun' was over. She was now thirty-six, and younger faces began to appear at the CSA center in Ottawa.

Occasionally, she returned to Houston to handle CapCom duties at Mission Control. She was later appointed Chief Astronaut of the Canadian Space Agency, and though it was a great job, Anna knew it also meant she was probably never returning to space.

Three years ago, when Howard Tyler had called her, Johnson initially thought it was a prank. *Miss Johnson, we'd like you to come back to Houston and take another physical.*

It wasn't until she passed the physical that NASA told her this wasn't going to be a trip to the International Space Station or a few orbits around the Earth in the new CEV.

You are on the short list for the prime crew of Mars 1. We want you to train for the pilot's seat on the MEV.

Johnson was stunned. *What is the MEV?* She asked.

The Mars Entry Vehicle. It's a two-stage lander, sort of like the old LEM we used on Apollo, but larger. Your job would be to get the crew to the Martian surface safely, perform scientific tasks for up to four months, and then get everyone back into Mars orbit for the trip home.

I see, she replied. *Count me in.*

Her Canadian pride overflowed to bursting and she immediately called her friends and family with the news.

Two weeks after that, Mission Commander Michael Walker, Mission Specialist Dale McKendrick, and Mars Entry Vehicle pilot Anna Johnson met for the first time. The three astronauts shook hands and sat down in Howard Tyler's office.

Anna's elation turned to anger and resentment almost from the moment she took her seat.

Michael Walker began by giving Anna a piercing look. "I have to go on the record here," he said. "I object to having Miss Johnson assigned to the prime crew. A woman on a three-person mission of this length would be an unnecessary distraction, and a serious risk. We need three men, not two men and a woman."

Johnson's heart raced, as she could hardly believe her ears. The mission commander was already trying to have her scrubbed on a flimsy sexist argument, and they had just met.

"No offense," Walker continued, "but this mission requires the maximum from everyone." He looked at her. "I don't think you can cut it mentally or physically."

Anna nodded. "I suppose so."

"So you agree with me, then?"

"Yes. I agree that this mission will require the maximum from everyone," she said. "I also believe I can keep up with either of you in every category that counts. I don't see a problem with me, only with your chauvinism."

"This isn't about chauvinism," said Walker. "It's practicality."

"And I say you're wrong," Johnson snapped back. "There is nothing shabby about my skills."

"You think you can pilot the MEV?" Walker said. "It's twice the size of the Apollo LEM and a lot more complex. I want someone with more flight experience to…"

"My flight experience is extensive, Commander Walker," Anna interrupted coldly. "I'm certain I can learn to handle the MEV. How can you judge my abilities on a spacecraft no one has even seen yet?"

Howard Tyler held up a hand. "Enough! Both of you please stop." He shook his head. "I've already heard this argument from other corners. The answer is no. Johnson is on the prime crew."

Mike Walker left his chair and went over to a wall displaying the pictures of all the astronauts who had died in the line of duty. He turned his back on everyone in the room and stared at the faces in their small chrome frames. He was surprised to discover he did not recognize some of them, and made a mental note to look them up later. "Johnson, do you know any of the people in these pictures?"

"Of course I do, sir. One of them is from Canada, you know."

"Well, if Dale and I can't depend on you to do your job, all three of us will end up with our pictures on this wall." He turned and bored his dark eyes into hers. "I'm warning you right now. I'm going to work your tail to the bone. You had better be able to keep up. Until you show me otherwise, you are just a showpiece assigned to this mission because you happen to be a Canadian astronaut. All our lives depend on your skills, and I have doubts about those skills. You haven't been in space for almost five years."

Anna was about to give him a sharp retort when Tyler interrupted.

"We chose her because she's the best astronaut in the Canadian Space Agency," he said, "*not* because she happens to be from Canada. And her gender is not an issue with NASA."

"We'll see," said Walker. He stared at Johnson like an ant he wanted to crush under his shoe.

Over the next thirty-six months, Walker kept his promise and demanded the absolute best from both Johnson and McKendrick. He worked them physically and mentally, driving them to the limits of human endurance, although he was much harder on Johnson. Much to his frustration, the harder he pushed her, the more she excelled. As the launch date approached, he realized she wasn't going to quit, no matter what he did.

Therefore, he added some extra salt tablets to her water bottles and waited for her to fail the cross-country exercise in the Nevada desert. It would be all the excuse he needed to convince NASA they should drop her at the last moment and assign her backup to the Mars 1 crew.

Johnson's backup was a man, of course, and a friend of Walker's.

Johnson startled and awoke to the clicking sound of the hatchback opening on the Jeep. She twisted around in the passenger seat and saw Mike Walker rummaging through the supplies in the back. Their eyes met. She saw a look of disappointment on his face.

"You made it here first. Good job," Walker said grudgingly. "Where's the debriefing team?" He dug through the boxes some more and grabbed a bottle of water and a ration pack.

"New orders. We have to get back to Nellis and catch a jet to Cape. Tyler wants to see us. Something about a problem with the cargo module."

"Great." Walker shut the hatchback with a loud bang and

climbed into the driver's seat, shutting the door. "How long have you been here?"

"Not too long."

"McKendrick?" Walker ripped open the ration pack and started eating.

"He should be here any minute." She noticed, strangely, that Walker wasn't drinking any water with his meal.

Walker grunted and swallowed a piece of beef jerky.

A suspicion began to form in her mind. She opened the door and stepped from the Jeep. "I'll be back in a minute."

"Sure." He continued eating.

Johnson walked to the back of the vehicle and saw Walker's pack sitting on the ground. She knelt down and swiftly examined the contents. There were still three full bottles of water in his pack even though the rules for the exercise had called for each astronaut to carry only two bottles.

Cheating bastard, she thought. *Bet he started out with a half-dozen.* She closed the pack.

The door to the warehouse swung open, and a tall man dressed in white coveralls entered. He waved to Anna and took off his New York City Marathon baseball cap, revealing a shiny bald head with short hair running around the sides that was beginning to gray. "Am I the last one here?" he said.

"Yes," Johnson said. She stepped away fro Walker's backpack. "Not by much. Mike showed up just a few minutes ago."

McKendrick nodded. "So you got here first? Nice going, Anna. Where's the debriefing team?"

"They were cancelled out. We've been ordered back to Cape right away."

"Oh yeah?" McKendrick said. "Why?"

"Problem with the cargo module or something." She popped the hatchback and pointed to the food and water. "Help yourself."

"Thanks." He snatched a couple of water bottles and leaned against the Jeep. He twisted the cap from one of the bottles and drank deeply. "Man, that's good."

"Hey, look. The old guy made it," said Walker from the front seat. "You didn't cheat and use your power scooter, did you?"

McKendrick laughed. "I'm an oldie but a goodie, baby. Damn, I wish they'd do desert training down by Vegas instead. At least we could hit the dinner buffet at the MGM Grand afterwards." He tore open one of the MRE's and examined the contents before tossing it aside with a wry expression. "Tell you one thing; I'm glad this is the last desert exercise on the training schedule."

"You should try it in the summer," said Walker.

"Funny guy, you are. It *is* summer." McKendrick twisted the cap on another water bottle and drained it in a few seconds. He gave a soft whistle of relief. "I needed that."

"Let's get back to Nellis," Walker said. "You two go over and pull that big sliding door open."

"In a minute," said Anna.

"We have to go, Johnson."

"I want to show you something, Mike. Come back here for a minute, please."

Walker stepped out and walked around to the rear of the Jeep. "Okay, what is it?"

Without warning, she slammed a palm into Walker's chest, shoving him against the Jeep. Her face was inches from his nose. "Did you think you were going to get away with it?"

Walker stared at her, saying nothing.

"Answer me!"

He grabbed her wrist and flipped it away. "What the hell's eating you? You think I've been pushing you too hard?"

"If you two want to punch it out," said McKendrick in a subdued voice, "perhaps you should put on boxing gloves first." He stepped between them. "On second thought, just cool it."

Walker and Johnson glared at each other in bitter silence.

Johnson's eyes flashed in anger. "I'm sick of this macho crap. We've been training together for three years, and still neither of you trusts me to do my job." She thrust a finger at Walker. "You never wanted a woman on this mission, Mike. Well, I have news for you. Grow up and get used to it. I'm here until NASA says otherwise."

"That can be arranged," said Walker.

"What exactly is it about me you don't like?"

"The truth? You're impulsive and stubborn," said Walker. "And I don't think you can pilot the MEV without overshooting our target or crashing into a crater wall. You've had six fatal errors already in the MEV simulator. Frankly, I'm just not convinced I should trust our lives to you." He looked over at McKendrick for support. "You have an opinion here, Dale?"

McKendrick spoke in measured tones. "She's had three successful sessions since those failures. Hey, we all crapped out on that thing the first few times."

"Will you two please stop talking about me like I'm not here?" Johnson said. "It's rude. You know perfectly well what's eating me, don't you Mike?"

Their eyes met, but Walker remained silent.

"Ask him about the water, Dale." She said.

"What's she talking about?" said McKendrick. "What water?"

"I don't know," said Walker.

"You don't exactly play fair, Mike," said Johnson.

"Take it easy, Anna." McKendrick held up his hands in a peace gesture. "I don't know what's going on here between you two, and it's true that Mike and I have had doubts about you, but I haven't voted to replace you on the crew. Not yet."

Johnson moved closer to McKendrick, as if she were sizing him up for a punch in the nose, as well. "Every time we work together, you two are picking my every move apart or making those stupid sexist jokes. The stress you create for me is incredible. Both of you need to back the hell off and let me do my job."

"Then do your job and do it right," Walker said.

A slight breeze passed through the building, creeping in through the cracks in the walls and cooling the air.

"I'm doing the best I can. I *can* get us to the Martian surface. I *can* fly the MEV," said Johnson. "I only want a fair chance. Even if I stepped aside for my backup, would you trust him enough to take over my job at the last minute?"

There was a long silence.

"Okay," said Walker at last. "It's a deal. *For now.* If at any time I think you can't do the job, I'll vote to put your backup in the left seat and take our chances. Now let's get going."

"Fair enough." She kicked at Walker's pack and met his eye firmly. "Don't forget your stuff."

Glitch

When Walker, McKendrick, and Anna Johnson touched down at Cape Canaveral, they were immediately hustled into Howard Tyler's office for a briefing on the cargo module. After Tyler finished explaining the problem, Walker shook his head in disbelief. "Does this mean a launch scrub?"

"Not necessarily," said Tyler. "We're working on ways to deal with it. We have to wait and see what happens when the module reaches Mars. There's no telling what it will do when it arrives in orbit. The onboard computer may crash completely and then so will the module."

"Any options being discussed?" asked McKendrick.

"A few," said Tyler. "MEP and JPL sent me a report with some recommendations. They think the module will slingshot around the planet on its aerobraking maneuver and then go for an immediate landing. If we can keep it in orbit until you arrive, one of you could go EVA and load some new software through a data port. It should accept commands from Houston after that."

"And if you can't keep it in orbit?" Walker said.

"Well, one idea being proposed is for you to do a longer burn with the *Abraham Lincoln's* main engine, make up the ten days the module will reach Mars ahead of you, and try to rendezvous with it just as it arrives."

Anna Johnson ran her hands through her hair and stared out the window. "Has anyone checked the fuel numbers on this extra burn?"

"Hell," said McKendrick, "I can tell you in two words. Not good. To make up a full ten days, we would have to do a burn on the main engine at least four extra minutes."

"That's nearly all of the reserve fuel," said Johnson.

"It's about three-quarters of the estimated reserve," said Dr. Tyler.

"What about course-corrections?" Johnson said sharply. "We may need that fuel for any extra corrections. You can't expect us to hang our butts out there because of a computer glitch on that module. If we burn our extra fuel playing catch-up with the MCM, we may not have enough left to hit our entry angle on the way home. You know what that means on an aerobraking capture, sir. We'll simply bounce off into space or burn up in the atmosphere. No rescue. No recovery. End of story."

"We're working on the fuel problem," Tyler said. "You would still be within mission parameters, even with the extra burn. And as far as a Mars landing, even if the cargo module fails completely, you can remain on the surface for about ten days on the short mission scenario. No one wants the short mission, I know. But it would be better than complete failure."

"Let's just hope we don't have to make too many course-corrections," said Johnson.

"Okay, it's your lives on the line here," said Tyler. "If you think it's too much of a risk, just say the word and I will scrub the mission until…"

Johnson shook her head. "No! Right now, we have the shortest window to Mars in years. If we miss this chance, it's going to take a lot more time and a much bigger fuel load to get there. This is our best shot for at least the next five years."

"What about it, Dale? What do you think?" Tyler said.

"I say we go," said McKendrick. "Ten days on Mars, or four

months, either way I am for going ahead."

"The situation could be more ideal," said Walker, "but I'm willing."

"All right, then. I wanted to hear it from all of you personally." As he shook each of their hands in turn, Tyler saw a strange, unspoken expression among the three astronauts as they left the office. He did not recognize the significance of it until later.

It was a fleeting look of doubt.

Tyler spent the rest of the afternoon consulting with the senior administrators at MEP by telephone. They quickly made a bold recommendation: *Move up the launch by ten full days.*

This plan meant a shorter burn from the main engine for the catch-up maneuver, and saved critical fuel. It also enabled the *Abraham Lincoln* to reach Mars orbit a full day before the renegade cargo module.

Tyler authorized the plan immediately. Mars 1 would launch in four days. He picked up the phone for one final call.

"White House operator. How may I direct your call?"

"Dr. Howard Tyler. For the President, please."

"Please hold a moment, Dr. Tyler."

The line clicked. "Hello, Dr. Tyler. What can I do for you?"

"Thank you for taking my call, Mr. President. I wanted to update you about some changes in the Mars mission schedule."

"Problems?"

"Yes. We've moved up the launch date by ten days."

"Why?"

Tyler explained the problem with the cargo module, and the solution proposed by the Mars Exploration Program team.

"Doesn't this pose more risk for the astronauts? Having to try and fix this module in Mars orbit?"

"I've spoken to the astronauts, Mr. President. They still want to try, even with the added risk. If they can't do the repair on the cargo module, then we go to what's called the short mission program. They would attempt a landing at Chrysse Plain, the same place one of the Viking Landers set down in 1976. Of course, without the supplies from the module, they could only stay on the surface for perhaps ten days." Tyler spoke more firmly. "Sir, even going to the short mission, we can learn more about Mars in ten days with working astronauts than from all of the unmanned probes we've sent previously."

"You don't have to convince me, Dr. Tyler. I have full faith in the program. I know you'll make the right decisions."

"We'll try not to let you down, sir."

"The entire world is praying for your success, you know."

"I hope so, Mr. President. I think some people would enjoy seeing us fail."

"Those people don't count, Dr. Tyler."

"Yes, sir. Are you still planning to attend the launch?"

"Wouldn't miss it for anything. I'll be there."

"Thank you, sir."

"You're welcome. Is that all?"

"Yes, sir."

"Thanks for the update. I'll see you in Florida." The line disconnected with a soft click.

Tyler made one more telephone call, this time to Jim Morris. When Morris came on the line, Tyler ordered him to inform the crew about the new launch date.

Anna Johnson sat at the dining table in her private quarters at Cape Canaveral and flipped through the pages on a heavy loose-leaf notebook. The book was secured with three metal rings big enough to fit over her wrist. It was NASA's 662-page DRM 16.0, or more simply, the Mars 1 mission plan. She had studied the manual for two and a half years, yet she never grew tired of it. It was a complex document, carefully written by the brain trust at MEP and Cal Tech. It detailed everything about the mission, even the basic housekeeping chores necessary in the Transhab during the long voyage to Mars.

Jim Morris had called a few minutes ago telling her about the decision to move up the launch. This was no surprise. She had wondered if MEP would suggest it. If it was a question of leaving earlier and saving fuel, or burning most of it in a shaky catch-up maneuver, she was in favor of leaving earlier and saving fuel.

She imagined for a moment what was going on at the Mission Planning office. *They're probably scuttling around like mice. The engineers and techs will be doing shifts around the clock.*

She took another sip of juice and flipped a page. Her favorite part of the book was that happy section at the end about a successful splashdown off the Florida coast. This was supposed to happen exactly 390 days after the *Abraham Lincoln* fired its first three SRB's and escaped from Earth orbit. The mission schedule called for eighteen weeks each way in transit and one hundred and twenty days on the Martian surface. *One year and a couple of weeks*, she thought.

The extended length of time in space did not worry her in the least. The cosmonauts on the old MIR space station had stayed in orbit for up to eighteen months at a stretch. The historical nature of the mission was always in the back of her mind, but neither did it make her hesitant. She turned another page and studied the schedule for Mission Day 135. That was 'Mars orbital capture' day. It was a polite term for plowing into the Martian atmosphere at over 17,000 miles an hour and roaring around the planet like a freight train on fire.

Johnson pushed the thought from her mind and concentrated on another part of the manual.

'We Hardly Ever Screw Things Up'

D ale McKendrick rolled out of his bunk at three-thirty in the morning and headed for the bathroom. He had found only a fitful sleep, overflowing with dreams about his wife and sons. Mission rules had separated him from his family for the last three days, but he knew they would be flying down from Atlanta today to watch the launch.

He scrubbed his face in cold water until he was fully awake and then stared hard at his reflection. He felt strong, but the face in the mirror was forty-six years old and so was the body. Staying in shape for the mission had required him to find physical reserves he never knew he possessed.

I'm the luckiest guy in the world, he thought.

He took a long, leisurely shower, enjoying the steamy sting of the hot water that magically made his aches disappear.

He was under no illusions. He knew why NASA had selected him for Mars 1, and it was not for his physical abilities. He had logged the most time in space of any active astronaut, having ridden two of the last three Space Shuttle missions before they were retired, as well as three missions on the new Crew Exploration Vehicle. *Experience,* he thought. *That's what they wanted for the third seat.*

He toweled dry and dressed from a neat stack of clothes prepared the night previously. He checked each item of clothing carefully, even though NASA technicians would soon have him undressed again and climbing into a pressure suit.

McKendrick allowed himself a smile in the mirror. *I must have been good in a previous life.* He took a few deep breaths and stretched. Some of his bones cracked. He checked his watch. It was time to go.

At exactly nine in the morning, the gantry elevator carrying Walker, Johnson, McKendrick, and two NASA technicians began its long climb to the White Room. The White Room was high above the ground and attached to the Crew Exploration Vehicle.

The three astronauts were dressed in pressure suits and carrying their helmets under one arm.

Anna Johnson tapped McKendrick on the shoulder and pointed into the distance. A large crowd of spectators had found spots in the official bleachers some distance away. Most of them were family members, government officials, dignitaries, or members of the media. A nonstop light show erupted from thousands of flashing cameras.

Walker took a brief glance at the crowd. "Nice turnout this morning. Must be something big going on today," he joked.

The elevator came to a stop. After some last-minute preparations in the White Room, they entered the CEV through the main hatch.

They were greeted by the CEV crew for the transfer, Alison Rogers and Ben Smith.

"Ready to go to Mars?" asked Rogers, smiling.

Walker shook her hand warmly. "You bet." He winked at Ben Smith. "Hey, rookie. How many hours do you have in this tub?"

"More than you, Mike. Don't worry. We hardly ever screw things up around here."

"That's right," Rogers said. "And no one will today, either. Let's make history."

The preflight technicians entered the cabin and strapped Johnson, McKendrick, and Walker tightly into their couches. They helped each of them put on their helmets and made sure they were secure. As they exited through the main hatch, one of the techs used a clean white rag to wipe around the seal.

Rogers and Smith gave everyone a thumbs-up and headed up to the flight deck.

Walker checked the large LED countdown clock mounted on the forward bulkhead. It read one hour and fifty minutes until launch. He heard a thump as the outer hatch was sealed.

Jim Morris stood by the main window in Launch Control and gazed across the concrete at the *Ohio*. White plumes of fuel vapor seeped slowly from pressure valves near its base. In the background, he heard the litany of back-and-forth communications between the launch controllers and the crew of the *Ohio*. The minutes ticked down until launch. It was now T-minus five minutes and counting.

Morris was excited, but in a subdued way. He knew this launch was only the first in a series of steps on a hazardous road.

He reached for another antacid to calm his churning stomach and chewed it just enough to gulp it down.

One hold had already been instituted when heavy black cloud passed over the Cape. The threatening weather had moved on and the countdown had resumed. Morris gave a slight nod to Launch Control supervisor Chris Wilkinson.

Wilkinson began calling over the intercom to different controllers, asking each if their particular station was 'go-for-launch'.

Morris had heard the droning litany a hundred times before, but this time he found himself listening more sharply.

CapCom...go...Flight...go...EECOM...go...Booster...go...

Wilkinson received a 'go' from all launch controllers. It was not a surprise. At this stage, most problems would have been discovered earlier, and a temporary hold instituted, or the launch scrubbed for the day.

"T-minus thirty seconds."

Morris continued watching the *Ohio* from the window. "God be with you all," he whispered.

"Eight...seven...six...main engine start..."

The CEV rose majestically from the pad on a carpet of raging fire and white smoke and cleared the tower smoothly, gobbling a half-ton of fuel per second.

One minute later, the *Ohio* entered its roll program and reached 'max-Q'. This was the point where g-forces exerted their maximum intensity on the spacecraft as it fought to escape Earth's gravity and achieve orbit. The *Ohio* became a distant point downrange in the morning sky and finally disappeared from view for good.

Graham Richardson stared through the eyepiece of the tracking telescope provided him in the VIP area. The only evidence remaining of the launch was a crooked contrail that was beginning to twist and scatter in the soft Florida breeze. He watched it for a long time.

The *Ohio* coasted safely into low Earth orbit. On the flight deck, Ben Smith and Alison Rogers adjusted course to intercept the *Abraham Lincoln*. The mission schedule called for an immediate rendezvous and crew exchange. The *Ohio* would then shadow the *Lincoln* in orbit until the *Lincoln* fired its first three SRB's and left Earth orbit. This was a safety consideration, in case anything went wrong on the *Lincoln* before the trans-Mars burn. In that event, Walker, Johnson, and McKendrick could transfer back to the *Ohio* and the mission would likely be scrubbed.

Thirty minutes later, Rogers was first to spot the *Lincoln* visually, as a light shining brighter than the background stars. She pointed it out to Smith. "There it is, at eleven o'clock."

The distance closed between the two spacecraft.

Ben Smith was amazed at the magnitude of the *Abraham Lincoln*. "It's twice our size," he said reverently.

"It's beautiful," replied Rogers. In the center was the Transhab, the round 'tuna can' section where the astronauts would live and work for a total of ten months. Just forward was the two-stage MEV landing-and-ascent vehicle. A conical heat shroud surrounded it, coming to a point at the front of the spacecraft. The shroud would protect the MEV and the *Abraham Lincoln* from the very high temperatures generated during aerobraking into the Martian atmosphere.

Behind the Transhab was the Earth Return Capsule, covered by another metal shroud. At the very rear of the assembly was the largest piece of all, the Magnum rocket with its six attached boosters.

Smith snapped off quick bursts on the maneuvering jets and eased the *Ohio* closer. He read the words painted in bright red on the white shell of the Magnum stage.

MARS 1 UNITED STATES-CANADA

A picture of each country's flag was displayed after the phrase.

Rogers kept a running commentary with Houston Control, while Smith called the two-man skeleton crew already aboard the Mars spacecraft. "Lincoln, this is Ohio. Moving into transfer position."

"Standing by, Ohio," came the reply.

NASA had decided against fitting the Mars spacecraft with a docking platform that was compatible with the CEV. The engineers had considered it both an expensive luxury and an unnecessary burden for something that would only be used once. Every pound of weight saved on the *Lincoln* meant more fuel and oxygen for the Mars crew.

Walker, McKendrick, and Johnson would have to pull themselves along a fifty-foot line to reach the airlock door on the *Abraham Lincoln*.

The two astronauts already running systems checks aboard the *Lincoln* would then transfer to the *Ohio*, and the exchange would be complete.

"Lincoln, this is Ohio. Stand by for tether release."

"Roger that, Ohio. Foster is just outside the airlock. You are go for tether release."

Smith flipped a switch. A special gold-braided line attached to the CEV shot toward the *Abraham Lincoln*.

As the flashing line reached astronaut Tim Foster, he snagged it with an expert hand. He attached it to a special metal ring near the airlock door. "Line secured," he announced. "I am going back inside the spacecraft now."

"Roger that," replied Smith. "Keep a close eye on the crew during the transfer, please."

"Roger that. We've got a good view from here."

"Houston," Alison Rogers told Mission Control, "I am ready to assist the Mars crew for EVA and transfer."

"Roger your assist and transfer," was the quick reply. Houston Control was watching closely, but they could only wait and worry. It was up to the astronauts now.

Rogers floated back into the main crew cabin and pulled herself over to Walker's couch. "We're ready for transfer, commander." She unfastened his restraints. "All of you double-check those helmet seals," she said.

A few minutes later, all four astronauts had climbed through the short tunnel to the outer airlock.

"Opening airlock door." Rogers opened the outer door, and the astronauts moved to the exit.

Walker checked his suit again for any problems, found none, and waited for the other two to do the same. The three of them grabbed a handrail and moved toward the airlock opening until they found the gold tether. The *Abraham Lincoln* drifted above them like a long, silent sentinel.

Each astronaut grasped the line and secured a safety ring on their EVA suits to the tether. "No worries," said Rogers. "You've got another full hour of air and it's only a five-minute crossing. Godspeed to all of you." She stood aside and took a grip on a nearby handrail to watch the other three as they made the crossing over to the *Lincoln*.

"Thanks. Starting across," said Walker. He tugged on the line to gain momentum. He floated out of the cargo bay and started a hand-over-hand maneuver, pulling himself toward the *Lincoln*.

Johnson took the line in her hands and followed Walker. This was her first space walk in years, and the stunning view of Earth made her gasp. It was a dinner plate jewel of blue, white, and brown suspended in a black sky with stars like looked like diamonds. She forced herself to stay focused and began pulling herself along the gold line toward the *Abraham Lincoln.*

"Right behind you," said McKendrick.

Two minutes later, they reached the outer airlock door on the *Lincoln.* After a struggle, they managed to pull themselves and their bulky suits into the airlock passage.

McKendrick was the last to enter. He stretched an arm outside the hatch door and unhooked the tether still connecting them to the *Ohio.* "Ohio," he called. "Retract now." The tether wiggled as it was retracted back to the *Ohio.*

McKendrick sealed the outer hatch. Air roared into the tiny cabin, and within a few seconds, the airlock was pressurized.

The inner hatch opened. Astronauts Tim Foster and Elliot Bassett waited expectantly as the Mars crew removed their helmets.

"Everyone okay?" Foster asked.

"Yes," replied McKendrick for everyone.

Foster extended his hand. "Welcome aboard the *Abraham Lincoln.* We've got a lot of work to do."

The *Ohio* and the *Abraham Lincoln* remained side-by-side for the next six hours as Foster and Bassett updated the crew about what they had learned on their month-long shakedown of the spacecraft.

After they were finished, Foster and Bassett shook hands with the Mars crew and bid them good luck. The gold line flashed over again, and they made their way along it to the *Ohio.*

Although the three astronauts had trained extensively with the Mars spacecraft's systems, it was another twenty-two orbits before Mission Control gave permission for the *Lincoln* to break out of Earth orbit.

Walker, McKendrick, and Johnson climbed into the Earth Return Capsule, just below the deck of the Transhab and took their seats. They began working on the checklist for the trans-Mars injection burn. Most of the controls for the *Lincoln* were located in the ERC, because the return capsule would be the last piece of hardware used on the mission. A backup control system existed in the Transhab.

McKendrick studied the control panels from his center couch. He watched as one special clock ticked toward zero. "Coming up on TMI," he said. "Sixty seconds."

Walker was in the right hand seat. He stared at Johnson over in the left seat, the pilot's seat.

Johnson could feel Walker's eyes watching her every move. She ignored him and switched on her com. "Houston, standing by for Trans-Mars injection burn. We show T-minus forty seconds."

"Roger, Lincoln. Enable pre-start on SRB's one, three, and five."

Johnson reached up and snapped three switches closed. "Boosters one, three, and five are at pre-start. Two, four, and six are locked out. Green lights across the board. T-minus twenty seconds." She settled back in her seat and gripped the armrests. "Brace yourselves, guys."

At the zero mark, three of the strap-on boosters attached to the *Lincoln* blasted to sudden life, slamming everyone hard into their couches. The spacecraft shook heavily as the solid-fuel rockets thundered out nearly a half-million pounds of thrust, pushing them out of Earth orbit and on a fast course for the Red Planet.

The deafening roar made it difficult to communicate, but Johnson kept up a running commentary with Houston, although she could barely hear her own words. Her heart was pounding so hard it seemed it would crack through her ribcage. "Houston! We have max thrust on all SRB's!" She shouted. "All systems are go!"

The *Lincoln* smoothed out as they increased velocity. At last, the vibrations ceased while the boosters continued to burn.

Johnson glanced at their velocity indicator. It was already at 19,500 miles per hour and increasing. *I've never seen one roll up that fast,* she thought. *We must be accelerating at record speed.*

After three long minutes, the boosters finally exhausted their fuel and fell silent. "SRB jettison," Johnson called out as she activated another switch. With a series of staccato bangs, the three expended rockets were blown clear of the *Lincoln* by explosive bolts.

"Your SRB's are clear, Mars 1," said Mission Control. This meant the empty boosters were moving away at a safe angle, and no longer posed a danger. "Stand by for main engine ignition in five seconds."

The liquid-fueled Magnum rocket ignited. Again, terrific g-forces pinned the three astronauts into their couches, as if they were on an extreme roller coaster ride. The shaking reached a fever pitch, and yet all of the panel indicators remained steady in the green. Johnson struggled against the g-forces to reach another switch and finally closed it with an effort.

"TM-abort jettison," she said. Another loud bang shook the spacecraft as a rocket attached to the very forward section of the *Abraham Lincoln* shot away. If used in an emergency, it would have separated the habitat, the MEV lander, and the Earth Return capsule from the Magnum rocket, pulling the astronauts back into Earth orbit for recovery, a sea rescue – and failure.

The burn clock hit zero and there was silence in the cabin.

"Houston, we have main engine cutoff," said Johnson, breathing a sigh of relief. "Telemetry looks good. All systems are still go."

"Roger that, Lincoln. We show same. How about those fuel numbers?"

McKendrick took a quick glance from his center couch. "Seventy-eight percent fuel remaining," he said.

"Good job, Lincoln," came the quick reply from Mission Control. "We show same on the fuel. You're definitely below the curve and on your way to Mars. Godspeed and good luck to you."

McKendrick had noticed the tension between Johnson and Walker during the two engine burns. *A hundred and thirty four days could be a long time for these two in this tin can,* he thought. He unsnapped his harness. "Let's move into the hab and get out of these damn suits," he said gruffly.

Twelve hours after the *Abraham Lincoln* blasted its way out of Earth orbit, Graham Richardson waited in the wings of the White House

Press Room.

One of his darkest secrets was his ability to deliver inspiring speeches even though he was a hopeless victim of stage fright. He recalled his days knocking on doors in Denver, trying to handshake and smile his way to Congress. He had learned to hide his nervousness effectively.

"Ladies and gentlemen, the President of the United States..."

Richardson stepped up to the podium. The conference was being carried live by all the major networks.

"Thank you for coming today," he began. "Before I take any questions, I have a few words. This morning at 9:28 AM, Eastern Standard Time, the Crew Exploration Vehicle *Ohio* launched from Cape Canaveral. It rendezvoused in Earth orbit with the Mars spacecraft and transferred to it the three astronauts who will become the first human beings to set foot on another planet. They are Mission Commander Michael Walker, Mission Specialist Dr. Dale McKendrick, and Mission Pilot Anna Johnson from the Canadian Space Agency. The *Abraham Lincoln* has already performed what NASA calls an 'injection burn,' and the spacecraft is now on course for Mars."

He paused.

"When I asked NASA three years ago if we could put humans on Mars, they told me they didn't know for sure. Nevertheless, today America has taken a giant step for mankind even farther than Neil Armstrong's, and we are showing the world what America can do, and what is possible when people work together. I ask everyone to pray for the safety of the astronauts. They are pioneers in the truest sense of the word. Thank you. I will take your questions now." Richardson pointed to a brunette woman sitting in the second row.

The woman got to her feet. "Thank you Mr. President. Shelby Patterson, Washington Post. Sir, there are reports that Mars 1 was a thrown-together rush program, because of pressure from the White House to attempt a manned mission to Mars during your first term. How do you respond to these reports?"

"I did not *order* NASA to go to Mars," said Richardson firmly. "I only asked them if it was *possible*. My decision to commit us on this course was about opportunity and what I believe this country needs right now."

"Mr. President, many experts are saying that the Mars mission is an inordinate risk for the astronauts. Will NASA will be held responsible if the mission fails?"

"No," said Richardson quietly. "That responsibility would be mine."

Breach

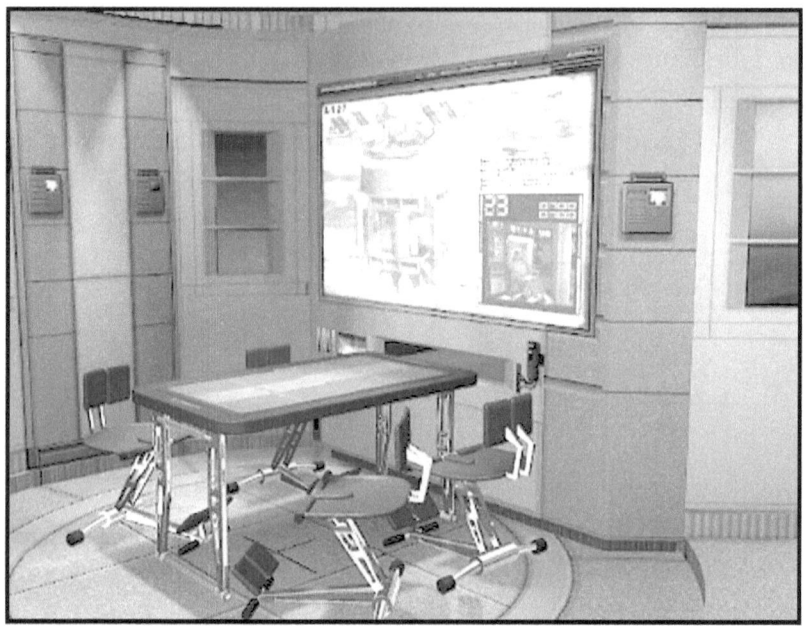

Mission Day 39

D ale McKendrick heard the insistent buzz of the wake-up alarm and reached for the shutoff button. He yawned, but remained under the covers for a few extra moments. McKendrick was already adjusting to life in the 'tuna can.' The ongoing end-to-end spin to create partial gravity for the hab had made him ill for the first day, but he had quickly adjusted to it.

His tiny cabin had a twin bed with storage compartments beneath it that also served as the bed frame. A child-sized desk table that folded down against the wall was the only other piece of furniture. Each cabin was two and a half meters wide at the broadest point. The wide point was against the far wall of the cabin, at the bed. The cabin narrowed to about one meter at the door. It was roughly in the shape of a pie slice. McKendrick quickly discovered that the cabin was the most precious space on the Transhab, because it was the only privacy available.

The designers had separated the sleeping quarters as much as possible, so that the three of them were located around the hab in a y-pattern. In between the cabins were the exercise cycle, a treadmill, a resistance-based weight lifting machine, the computer station for monitoring the ship's systems, and a cramped bathroom with shower, sink, and toilet. In the center of the cramped habitat was a tiny communal kitchen with food storage cabinets.

The entire hab was roughly four times the size of an average family room, with a claustrophobically low ceiling. A single ladder was mounted just outside the kitchen area. It was firmly attached to both deck and ceiling, with a hatch on both sides. The ceiling hatch led through a short tunnel into the MEV lander. The deck hatch dropped into the Earth Return Capsule.

The *Abraham Lincoln* was now in a gravitational rotation, turning end over end through space. This provided some artificial gravity, enabling the astronauts to move around without bouncing off the walls.

Strange creaking sounds emanated from the hull occasionally as the spacecraft settled into the rotation, but this was expected. It still made everyone a bit nervous.

McKendrick kept a personal log, and he included the dates and times of the noises. He noted they were happening more frequently. At this point, there was no need for concern. Nevertheless, he found himself keeping a closer eye, just in case.

The *Abraham Lincoln* had already traveled more than eight million miles from Earth. The moon was now only a very bright star and the Earth a blue-and-white jewel the size of a dime. The gravitational rotation created a star show of rolling lights as it passed by the windows.

"Dale?" Anna Johnson called over the intercom speaker.

McKendrick yawned and lifted his head from the pillow. "Yes?"

"I need you up in the MEV for a systems check in about ten minutes."

"On my way."

"Thanks." McKendrick rolled out of his bunk. A minute later, he was out the door and into the galley to grab a cup of coffee before going up to the MEV.

Someone, probably Johnson, had already made a pot and left it in the sealed container everyone used. The lower gravity made accidents more likely, and much of the galley equipment was designed with this fact in mind. McKendrick found a mug and a lid and carefully poured it full. He took a sip and nodded in approval.

A quick glance around the empty hab told him that Walker was still asleep in his own cabin.

Everyone kept a strict twenty-four hour routine, taking turns on housekeeping chores, maintenance checks, and drills. They rotated the watches, using the overlaps on their watches to keep an eye on each other.

The workload was immense. McKendrick knew he was not as sharp as he had been before they left Earth.

Everyone is tired, he thought.

He raised the mug and took another drink of the hot liquid. It rolled down his throat and woke him up a bit.

They all knew the score. The universal assumption was that dying was secondary to the bigger tragedy of failure. Getting yourself killed was bad enough, but screwing the pooch would be far worse.

McKendrick checked his watch and finished his coffee. It was a couple of minutes until Johnson needed him up in the MEV. Walking over to a bank of monitors and control boards against the outer wall of the hab, he scanned the readouts with an expert eye. Nothing seemed out of the ordinary. Sitting down at the single chair provided, he began running some system analysis checks through the computer.

He noticed a slight fluctuation in air pressure inside the short tunnel that connected the hab to the MEV lander. *Now, that is strange*, he thought. Checking another readout, he saw that the *Abraham Lincoln's* computer was attempting to repressurize by forcing occasional shots of compressed air into the tunnel. He switched on the intercom link to the MEV lander. "Anna?"

"Go ahead."

"You'd better get down here."

"What's the problem?"

"Pressure in the tunnel is falling. There may be a leak. The computer keeps doing a repress in there. Check the pressure readout before you try to come through. Make sure it's safe."

"Okay. Give me a second."

A couple of moments later, the ceiling hatch dropped open and Johnson did a fireman's slide down the ladder. She pushed a button on the ladder and the hatch closed automatically. She hurried over to the control panels and stared over McKendrick's shoulder.

He pointed to a particular readout. "There. See it? The computer keeps trying to repress, but I think we're just sending atmosphere out into space. We may have taken a hit from a micrometeoroid."

"I think you're right," Johnson said. "I thought I heard air escaping when I came through the tunnel. Couldn't be sure, though."

They both watched the gauge intently for about a minute. It was up, then down, but steadily dropping.

"This is not good," said Johnson. She found the intercom switch for Walker's cabin. "Mike!"

"What is it?"

"Get your lazy ass out of bed. We're losing cabin pressure in the MEV tunnel."

Still dressed in a T-shirt and underwear, Walker stumbled sleepily from his cabin and ushered McKendrick away from the chair. He sat down and typed in a command.

The computer verified what the gauge was reading. The atmospheric pressure in the connecting tunnel between the MEV lander and the habitat was definitely falling.

"Suit up," said Walker. "We need to go in there and check..."

Without warning, a loud bang shook the habitat so hard the floor plating rattled. The spacecraft pitched hard, spilling all three of them to the deck. The lights vanished, plunging the cabin into darkness.

"Emergency lights!" shouted Johnson, trying to struggle to her feet. The spacecraft rolled wildly a second time and she was thrown to the deck again. She flung her arms out and grabbed the bottom of the chair. "Walker! Lights! Come on!"

McKendrick flew into the nearest wall, banging his shoulder. "Ow!" The master alarm erupted with a loud, intermittent buzz.

Walker was still sitting in the chair, one hand keeping a death grip on the armrest, while he fought to locate the control for the lights with his other hand. The deck pitched again and he was thrown from the seat and onto on his knees. He reached up and finally found the switch for the lights. "Got it!" Several wall-mounted lamps flashed to life. The hab continued to roll like some crazy amusement ride, followed by a terrible screeching noise. Walker was thrown headfirst into the control panels, and he collapsed to the floor. Blood from an ugly gash on his forehead flowed into his eyes.

Johnson crawled on her hands and knees, fighting to reach the seat Walker had recently vacated. She finally struggled into the seat. "We've got damage in the tunnel! We're pumping so much oxygen in there that the leak is pushing us out of alignment." She shut down the master alarm.

"Alert," said the computer over the loudspeakers. "Emergency power enabled. Pressure leak in MEV tunnel. Gimbal warning. Navigation alert."

"Computer! Stop repress to the MEV tunnel!" Johnson said.

"Affirmative," the computer replied calmly. "Ceasing repressurization to MEV tunnel. Entry hatches are sealed. Warning – there is now zero atmosphere in the MEV tunnel."

The pitching finally stopped, but the spacecraft was still rotating like a merry-go-round at high speed. Johnson focused on the controls, trying to fight her dizziness from the unchecked spin.

Walker lay on the deck, unconscious and still bleeding from the wound to his forehead.

McKendrick crawled across the deck toward him, working around the chair where Johnson was seated. He got behind Walker and grabbed him by the armpits. He pulled Walker's head into his lap and slapped a hand on the wound to staunch the bleeding. "Come on, Anna!" he said. "We're going to be torn apart if you don't get that spin under control!"

"Give me a couple of seconds." Instead of the slow, steady, end-to-end rotation that had provided artificial gravity, the *Lincoln* was now spinning rapidly on a flat axis. Johnson activated a control that ordered the navi-computer to halt the rotation. "Hold on, everyone," she said. "Here comes zero-g." Small thrusters mounted on the outside of the hull hissed in choppy bursts. The huge spacecraft gradually stopped its spinning.

Walker and McKendrick floated gently off the deck. The unconscious Walker's arms were spread as if he were welcoming a houseful of guests to a party. A look of peace shrouded his face. His eyes were closed.

"How is he?" asked Johnson.

McKendrick continued keeping his palm firmly against Walker's wound to control the bleeding. "He's unconscious but he's still breathing okay. I need help here, though."

"All right." Johnson checked to make sure their communications were still working, and then switched to the X-band transmitter. "Houston, Mars 1. Houston, this is Mars 1, do you read?"

The emergency lights flickered and grew dim. The ventilation fans rolled to a stop. It was silent as a cave in the habitat, and nearly as dark. Johnson watched helplessly as a signal-strength indicator on their com-system fell to zero. Communications were gone, at least for now.

The computer spoke again in a soft voice. "Main power unit failure. Auxiliary power unit enabled." The lights came on and the fans began humming once more.

"What the hell happened?" said McKendrick.

"The MEV tunnel is damaged," Johnson said. "Probably caused some short-circuits. That automatically triggers the safety breakers. The breakers are reset now, but it's a complete vacuum in the tunnel. We'll have to suit up and check the damage."

"Can you find the medical kit?" said McKendrick. "I can't take pressure off his head wound. He's got a pretty big cut on his forehead."

Johnson unsnapped her lap belt and floated away from the

chair. Using a swimming motion, she made her way to the central galley and retrieved the kit from a storage locker. Kicking her way back to McKendrick, she grabbed both men to steady herself. She hooked a leg over McKendrick's and opened the medical kit. She dug out a large bandage and peeled off the backing.

When McKendrick moved his hand away from the wound, a few globules of blood wobbled into the air like crimson Jell-O. Johnson pressed the bandage firmly into place. The bleeding stopped.

"If we're going to suit up to check the tunnel," said McKendrick, "we'll have to suit him up, too."

"Yes." She checked the readouts showing conditions up in the MEV. They were normal, but the access tunnel between the hab and the lander was now a complete vacuum. "Can you get him into his suit and move him up there by yourself?"

"I think so."

"Put him in couch three. Make sure you strap him in."

"Mars 1 this is Houston..." called an urgent voice over the loudspeaker.

Johnson knew there was approximately a forty-five second delay in their communications with Mission Control because of their current distance from Earth. *Houston is probably in panic mode right now,* she thought. They received a constant stream of telemetry and other data from the *Abraham Lincoln.* The data they were getting now would have them scrambling for answers. She had to give them what answers she could.

"Houston, this is Mars 1," Johnson said. "We have tunnel damage between the hab and the MEV. Commander Walker has suffered a head wound and a possible concussion. We have lost main power and have switched to auxiliary. Life-support is go, I repeat, life-support is still go. We have zero atmosphere in the MEV tunnel. Damage to tunnel unknown at this time but we are preparing to check it. Gravitational rotation has been shut down. We are in no immediate danger but the situation is critical and we are moving off-course rapidly. Check your telemetry and please advise. Out."

A few minutes later, McKendrick had finished dressing Walker's wound more thoroughly and getting him into his EVA suit. He donned his own suit and helmet and moved the still-unconscious man to the ladder leading up to the MEV.

Johnson was already in her suit. She depressurized the hab for the transfer to the MEV. She pulled the hatch open and helped McKendrick float Walker up into the narrow tunnel. She squeezed inside after him and opened the access door to the MEV. Together they managed to push him into the MEV cabin.

"I can do this," said McKendrick. "What did Houston say?"

"No answer yet. Probably in a panic right now. Let's finish this."

They pushed Walker down gently into the center seat and fastened his restraining harness.

"I think he's just knocked out," said McKendrick. "I checked his vitals. They're okay. He's going to need stitches, though. I'll do it."

"Stay with him after you're finished. I'll talk to Houston and then check that tunnel."

"Be careful."

"I will." She turned to go.

McKendrick put a hand on her shoulder. "This means end-of-mission, doesn't it?"

Johnson's face took on a determined expression. "Don't count us out yet, Dale. Let's see what Houston has to say first."

Go or No Go

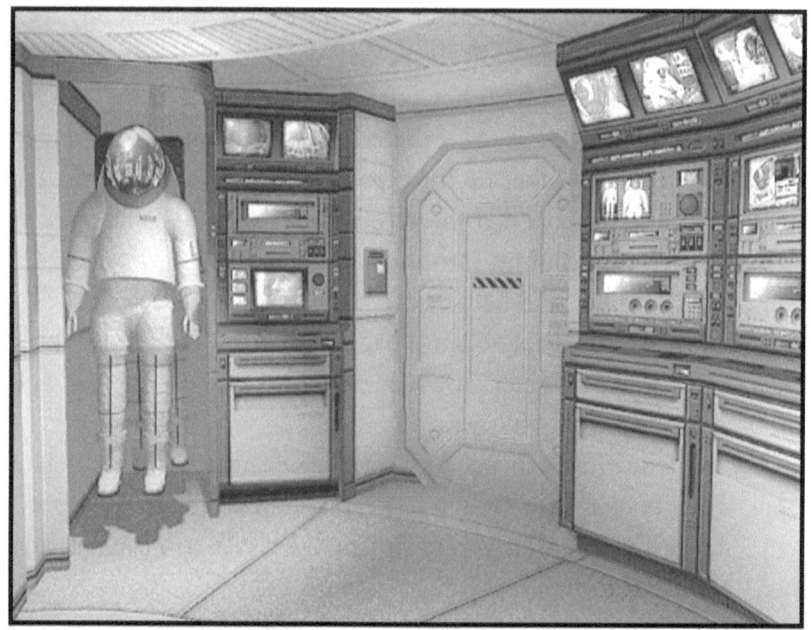

J ohnson examined the damage in the tunnel between the MEV lander and the habitat. She saw a tear in the hull about the size of a loaf of bread. The metal along the edges of the hole were twisted and stretched. She realized at once, what had happened to the *Lincoln*.

It was not meteoroid damage that had caused the tunnel to give way. It was the gravitational rotation, the end-to-end spin that had created artificial gravity for the spacecraft. The tunnel had been placed under too much stress, and the tunnel had failed. She switched on the exterior cameras from a small control panel nearby and scanned the outside damage from a video screen.

Two long bolts securing the tunnel to a supporting frame had been warped into grotesque shapes. The engineers had failed in their estimates of the stress created by the spacecraft turning end-over-end for months at a time. The rip in the hull was the result.

Johnson knew that even if the mission continued, the *Lincoln* had just become a zero gravity environment. *I can fix the hull damage,* she thought, *but we'll never be able to start up rotation a second time. Too risky.*

"Dale," she called over her suit radio. "Let's move back to the hab. Make sure you check Walker's helmet seals before you open the hatch. How is he? Is he awake?"

"Negative, Anna. He's still out cold."

"All right. Open the hatch when you're ready."

"Roger that."

She helped McKendrick pull Walker's unconscious form back through the tunnel and into the relative safety of the habitat. Once the hatch to the damaged tunnel was secured, she floated over to the monitors and restored cabin pressure to the habitat. Compressed air roared into the cabin. When a green light on the control panels showed full atmosphere had been restored, she pulled off her helmet and nodded toward Walker. "Can you get him out of his suit and make sure he's okay?"

McKendrick nodded and floated Walker into his cabin, using some handholds along the walls.

"You'll have to secure him to the bunk," she called after him. "Not too tight, though."

"No problem."

She opened a compartment and pulled out three sets of gray boots, and then activated the magnetic field in the deck plating of the habitat. When she dropped the boots to the deck, the field sucked them to the floor with a soft snap. She stepped into one set of boots and left the others in place.

She buckled herself into the control couch and made the call she dreaded, but knew Mission Control was frantically anticipating. "Houston, Mars 1. Stand by for damage report and current status." As she waited for her message to reach them, she wondered if Mission Control had already made the call to abort. Her mind raced with the possibilities. She ran their telemetry numbers through the navi-computer. They were far off-course. The forty-five second delay in communications was frustrating. She waited impatiently for a reply. Finally, a tense voice burst through the speakers.

"Mars 1, Houston. We show a dropout of telemetry for thirty-six seconds. Your present telemetry does not look good. You will have to perform a course-correction burn. Standing by for your status report."

Johnson told them everything she knew in a single long message, including the damage to the tunnel. She tempered this news by adding her opinion that the hull damage could probably be repaired and that chances were good an engine burn would do no further damage. Her message would start the decision-making process moving at NASA. The final call to abort or continue the mission would have to made quickly.

The *Lincoln* was moving farther off course every second.

I hope this isn't the end of it, she thought.

Jim Morris stood at the back of the Mission Control room with his arms folded. It had been nearly thirty minutes since the tunnel accident on the *Lincoln*. He studied some large video screen displays on the far wall with an expert eye. Each screen showed different data being relayed back to Earth from the spacecraft.

Morris had just returned from an emergency video conference with the MEP team at the Jet Propulsion Laboratory. After analyzing the data coming in from Mars 1 and reviewing all the options, they had made a quick recommendation: *Abort the mission immediately and bring the astronauts home.*

The MEP team had several reasons to recommend an abort and all of them were logical.

However, the final decision fell to Morris and Howard Tyler. It was a difficult call. The tunnel damage on the *Abraham Lincoln* was not necessarily critical; however, it was possible that firing the main engine for a course correction could cause more damage. Perhaps the stresses would tear the tunnel away and split the spacecraft completely in half, with the MEV lander flying away in one direction and the habitat in the other direction.

Morris ran the problem through his mind. *Well,* he thought, *they have to fire the engine anyway, whether to make the correction or turn back for home. So, that's not really a deciding factor.*

Howard Tyler stood stoically a few feet away. "Jim?"

"Yes."

"What do you think? There's not much time."

"I know." Morris checked his microphone. "FIDO?"

"Go Flight," came the quick response.

"How are they looking up there?"

"Not good, Flight," said the Flight Dynamics Officer. "They're tumbling close to gimbal lock."

"Guidance," Morris called.

"Go Flight."

"Status?"

"*Lincoln* is still go on all nav systems, Flight."

"PROP?"

"Go, Flight."

"Give me a fuel status for an immediate course correction."

"Flight, we have twelve minutes to get them back on course," said the Propulsion Engineer Officer from his console. "After sixteen minutes they'll be so far out of the corridor they won't have enough fuel to get home. We have to do an immediate burn or it's end-of-mission."

Morris considered this information for a few seconds. "CapCom!"

"Go, Flight."

"What's our current com delay?"

"Fifty seconds, Flight."

"Order Johnson to stand by for a course-correction burn. Tell her she has to execute the burn in less than ten minutes or everyone comes home."

The CapCom controller began relaying the urgent message.

Walker regained consciousness and groaned. He reached up and touched the bandage on his forehead. "Shit," he murmured.

McKendrick was sitting next to him. "Welcome back. Don't touch that bandage too much. You've got stitches in your head now."

"What the hell happened?"

"Decompression in the tunnel. You hit your head on one of the control panels."

At the same moment, Johnson opened the door to the cabin and stuck her head inside. "We have to move into the ERC and do a correction burn," she said. "*Now.*"

"How much time do we have?" McKendrick asked.

"Houston says we're down to less than ten minutes, otherwise we'll have to abort."

"Ten minutes? Sweet Jesus." McKendrick said. "Can we do this?"

"Yes. You okay, Mike?" Johnson asked.

"Yeah, yeah. My head hurts, otherwise I'm fine. Let's get down to the ERC."

Johnson held out two pairs of boots. "You'll need these."

They quickly made their way through the deck hatch and down into the Earth Return Capsule. They secured their restraints and started the required checklist for the burn.

The burn data arrived from Houston. Johnson switched on the navi-computer. "Computer is up…locking in burn data…" She flipped a row of switches closed above her head. "Fuel pumps on…pre-start…"

"Kick it in the butt," said Walker. "We're out of time."

"Navi-computer enabled. Ignition in five…four…three…"

"Never mind," said McKendrick.

The *Abraham Lincoln* roared to life like a dragon awakened from a long sleep. A tremendous vibration shook the capsule.

"What about the tunnel? Did Houston figure on the stresses?" shouted Walker.

"Too late to worry about that now!" Johnson yelled back at him.

When the roaring ceased two minutes later, Johnson checked their status and let her breath out in a soft whoosh. "The tunnel is still intact. And we're back on course." She stared at the fuel readings for the Magnum engine. They were down to less than twenty percent.

The new margin for error on the mission had just fallen to absolute zero.

Follow the Leader

December 13   Mission Day 135

McKendrick handed up the last of the white plastic boxes containing the Mars science packages to Walker. Walker took the box and carefully placed it into a storage locker aboard the MEV. He closed the locker and looked down at McKendrick. "Everything secure in the hab for separation?"

"All items completed on the checklist." McKendrick pulled himself up and floated into the lander. He sealed the hatch and climbed into his center couch. "Any problems?"

Johnson, already in the pilot's seat, pointed to a video screen. "Mars," she said. "And we're go on all systems."

The image filled the screen. McKendrick stared in awe at the tan color of vast deserts and the bright white of the Martian ice caps. "It's beautiful," he whispered.

"I agree. Time to go to work now, boys," she said. "Coming up on Mars capture interface. Two minutes. Pull in the camera, Mike."

"Roger that," said Walker. "Retracting camera. Any signal from the cargo module yet?"

"No," said Johnson. "We should have visual contact after our first orbit."

"Can we make rendezvous with it or not?"

"Yes. Houston says we'll have less than an hour to replace the software. After that, it will probably start Mars entry on its own. God knows where it will land."

"If it does," Walker said firmly, "we'll follow it down to the surface. We need those supplies."

Johnson said nothing. She knew that particular idea was extremely dangerous. "One minute to entry interface," she said.

As the *Abraham Lincoln*, protected by its heat shroud, angled into the Martian atmosphere, McKendrick was calm and completely relaxed for the first time in weeks. The last four months had been the toughest of his life. Every since the damage to the tunnel, Mission Control had ordered maximum time for everybody on the exercise equipment, to keep their muscles toned during the long period in zero gravity. This was in addition to the scores of other duties they had been forced to perform on the long voyage, including him and Johnson going EVA to seal up the damaged tunnel with a special epoxy.

Everyone was near exhaustion and stressed to the breaking point. Tempers had flared occasionally, albeit briefly. Fortunately, after the near-disaster with the MEV tunnel, there had been no other serious incidents. They had now arrived in Mars orbit.

It had been, as McKendrick had predicted, a very long four months.

"Interface," said Johnson.

The *Abraham Lincoln* slammed into the Martian atmosphere at five miles a second. As the ablating material burned away on the aeroshell, the spacecraft left a fiery trail across the sky, like a comet.

Back at Mission Control in Houston, the flight controllers watched the big screen as a computer-generated image of the spacecraft moved slowly around an image of Mars. A string of numbers above the screen constantly changed, showing the velocity, angle, and position of the *Abraham Lincoln*. The spacecraft was now in a temporary communications blackout until it emerged from the far side of the planet.

Around the world, people gradually stopped whatever they happened to be doing, and started gathering in front of televisions and radios. The streets of nearly every major city on Earth began to empty, as the human race turned its complete attention to the drama unfolding millions of miles away on another planet.

Nearly fifty years before, it had been Neil Armstrong and his small step for man, or perhaps Apollo 8's Christmas wish from lunar orbit that had brought the world together.

Today it was Mars 1.

The astronauts sat calmly in the cabin of the MEV lander and watched the control panels for any problems as the *Lincoln* thundered through the upper Martian atmosphere. The awful roaring from the aerobraking finally began to ease as they exited the atmosphere and headed out into space. Then the hand of Mars gravity reached out and pulled them back into a stable orbit around the planet. The vibrations died away and all was silent again.

"We're clear of blackout," said Walker.

"Houston, Mars 1," said Johnson. "Aerobraking maneuver complete. Mars orbit achieved." She thought for a moment. "Houston, we still need that telemetry on the cargo module for the rendezvous."

"We're down to forty minutes before it begins Mars entry," McKendrick reminded her gently.

Walker held up a small disk the size of silver dollar. "Just get us close enough to load this software," he said, "and we can call Mars home for the next four months." He placed the disk into a special insulated container and handed it reverently to McKendrick.

McKendrick tucked it gently into a leg pocket on his pressure suit, zipping the pocket closed. "Time to get ready," he said. He pushed away from the couch and floated toward the airlock door. He freed the snaps holding his portable life-support pack to the wall.

Walker followed him and helped him secure the pack to the back of the pressure suit. "You up to this?"

"You bet." McKendrick had wanted to do the installation, anyway. He had the most experience working in space, and made no bones about the fact. It made sense that the job be assigned to him. He checked his connections between the PLSS backpack and his suit. They were solid.

He gave Walker a thumbs-up and moved into the airlock.

Walker returned the gesture and sealed the inner door.

"I've got the module's tracking radar," said Johnson, staring intently at the controls. "I'm feeding it into the navi-computer now."

A voice from Mission Control spoke from the cabin speakers. "Mars 1, Houston. Copy your message. You should have a visual on the target in less than eight minutes. Good luck."

"Thank you, Houston," replied Johnson. "McKendrick is standing by in the airlock for the EVA."

McKendrick peered out into space from a tiny window set into the outer door of the airlock. "Anna?" he called out on his suit radio.

"Go ahead, Dale."

"I'm ready at the outer hatch. Panel tool secured. Software disk secured."

"Roger that. Seven minutes to rendezvous position. I have the module on radar now. Don't forget to check your helmet seals again before opening the hatch."

"Roger." McKendrick ran some numbers through his mind. They had about thirty minutes before the cargo module started down to the Martian surface on its own accord. Johnson had said they would be in position within seven minutes. That meant a scant twenty-three minutes for him to make his way over to the module and load the new software. *Too little time*, he thought. It was Murphy's Law of space work: *Everything takes longer than you expect.*

"Dale?"

"Go ahead."

"Stand by for aeroshell jettison."

"Roger." McKendrick took a firm hold with both hands on a nearby handrail.

The conical panels that had blanketed the front of the *Lincoln,* protecting it from the intense heat of aerobraking, blew away with a loud thump. McKendrick peered out the viewing window and watched the white panels drift away from the *Abraham Lincoln* in two pieces. "Panels are moving away," he called.

"Roger. How do they look?" she asked.

"I can see black streaking and some burn marks. No obvious damage, though."

"That's good news," said Johnson. "Means the aeroshell on the ERC will probably work when we get home, too. Okay. Stand by for MEV separation."

"Roger."

Johnson flipped up the plastic cover on a red switch marked MEV-SEP.

She pressed the button and the MEV lander fairly jumped away from the *Abraham Lincoln* with a soft bang. "We're loose," she said. "Houston, we have MEV sep. We are pitching around." Firing small bursts from the control rockets, she positioned the lander at the correct angle. She restored control to the navi-computer again for the rendezvous with the cargo module. Other control rockets on the lander began to fire intermittently in tiny bursts.

"Two minutes to rendezvous point," she said.

The tension at Mission Control was thick as tar. Jim Morris watched the screen graphics and listened carefully to the delayed transmissions from the *Lincoln.* The com-delay factor was frustrating for everyone. He stood in the back of the room with his arms folded akimbo. Next to him was Howard Tyler.

"Think they can make the software switch in less than thirty minutes?" Tyler asked.

"Maybe. Usually, we would schedule an hour and a half for a task like that."

"McKendrick's good."

"He's the best," said Morris. "But we're asking for a miracle here."

"It's a miracle they even reached this point," said Tyler.

"You got that right."

Anna spotted the cargo module out the viewing window on her left. It resembled the tank on a gasoline truck. The module was below and slightly ahead of the MEV. Beyond it, she saw the Martian surface, filling up the sky. She grasped the joystick controller, taking control back from the navi-computer, and eased the MEV closer.

"Two hundred at three," Walker announced. This was shorthand, informing her they were now two hundred meters from the module, and moving toward it at three meters per second.

"Roger." Johnson pulled the joystick toward her, slowing the MEV's velocity as it approached the target.

"One sixty at two," said Walker.

Johnson continued snapping the attitude jets expertly, until the two vehicles now floated in space side-by-side, only fifty meters apart. "We're in position," she called over the radio to McKendrick. "You are go for the EVA, Dale. Good luck."

"Roger that. Opening outer hatch now." McKendrick was wasting no time. Without hesitation, he pushed himself away from the MEV and into open space. He kept his eyes focused on the module and gripped the twin control handles on his backpack tightly. Squeezing the throttles, tiny spurts from gas jets pushed him toward the module. In less than a minute, he was approaching the access door on its starboard side. He utilized the jets once more to position himself within reach of a small panel.

"I'm at the access," he called.

"Roger that," replied Johnson. "Good job. We can see you from here, no problem."

McKendrick unsnapped a special holster on his leg and removed a stainless steel tool faintly resembling a skeleton key. Inserting it into a slot on the access door, he turned it to the right and opened the panel. He took out the data disk from the pocket on his leg. "I'm in," he said. "I see the slot. I'm inserting the disk."

Two lights flashed on a readout panel as he inserted the disk. "I have green lights," he said. "Data is loading."

"All right, Dale. Wrap it up and get back here," said Johnson. "That's all you can do."

"Closing the panel now," he answered. "It's done." He tucked the tool carefully into its holster. "On my way." He turned away and fired his suit jets.

McKendrick was halfway to the MEV when a strange feeling made the hairs on his neck stand on end. He turned his head with some difficulty and glanced back at the cargo module.

The two heat-shield panels on the forward end of the module were beginning to open like a flower in morning bloom. "Shields are deploying on the module!" McKendrick shouted. He turned away and gave his suit jets a hard burst toward the MEV.

"No!" Walker shouted in frustration from his seat in the MEV. "It's too soon!" His voice was a roar in everyone's headsets.

"Quiet down," Johnson said. "Both of you. Don't overload your mikes. You're just breaking up. Dale, get back inside here now!"

"I'm almost at the airlock," he replied.

"What the hell's going on out there?" Walker said. He turned his attention to checking the MEV's systems. "We still had ten minutes at least."

Johnson watched the module from her window. "I don't know, Mike. But that thing is going to fire its descent engine in less than a minute and Dale is still out there."

"Take it easy, Anna. I'm already inside the airlock," said McKendrick over the radio. "Outer hatch is sealed. Go ahead and repress."

"Roger." Johnson reached up and activated a control to repressurize the airlock. Compressed air roared into the passage.

"We're following the module down to the surface," said Walker. "Start tracking its new telemetry."

"I think we should discuss that plan first, Mike." Johnson said.

"That's an order." He unsnapped his harness and floated over to the airlock door to assist McKendrick.

Johnson craned her neck and called after him, "What if it decides to land in a boulder field? Have you considered that?"

"Then you'll have to find us the best site you can within a couple of kilometers of wherever it lands! You're wasting time. Lock on its telemetry and put us on the identical course." Walker pulled the inner airlock hatch open and helped McKendrick inside.

McKendrick removed his helmet. "Did the best I could," he gasped. "What happened?"

"Don't know," said Walker. "It went into the entry program a few minutes early, that's all. Probably another glitch in the software or something. Bad luck, I guess."

"What does Houston say?" McKendrick asked.

"We're following the module down to the surface," said Walker.

The two men took their seats.

"That's not from Houston," said Johnson. "Mike made the call."

"Is that right?" McKendrick said. "Can we do it safely?"

"We can't wait for Houston to decide," said Walker. "By that time we'll be halfway through another orbit. We have to stay on that module's tail or we'll lose it."

McKendrick said nothing.

Johnson checked their com-signal. It was strong. "Houston, Mars One. MCM has gone into Mars entry program ahead of schedule. The software installation has failed. Repeat. That is a negative on the software. We are locked on its telemetry and following it to the surface." She glanced over at Walker and added, "This is on Commander Walker's direct order."

Walker stared right back at her and nodded firmly.

Johnson typed in commands telling the navi-computer to track the course of the module and attempt a landing in the same area. At that moment, the cargo module suddenly fired its rockets and fell away toward the Martian surface.

"There it goes," said McKendrick.

The navi-computer automatically fired the descent engines on the MEV lander with a giant roar, giving chase.

"Dammit!" Jim Morris shouted in frustration as Johnson's latest transmission reached Mission Control. "What in the hell is he doing?" Everyone in the room knew that Walker was taking a huge risk by rejecting the short mission program and trying to follow the module down to the surface instead.

The short mission meant an easy touchdown on Chrysse Plain, a look at an old Viking Lander, but only ten days on Mars.

Morris understood exactly why Mike Walker was rolling the dice. The mission commander was trying to extend the mission.

They won't have long to find a good landing site on their limited fuel supply, Morris thought. The crew had few options now. If something went wrong during the landing, they would have to dump the bottom half of the lander and then fire the upper stage engines and climb back into Mars orbit. After that, they would rendezvous with the *Abraham Lincoln* and head for home. Failure this close would be hard on everyone.

Canyons and Mountains

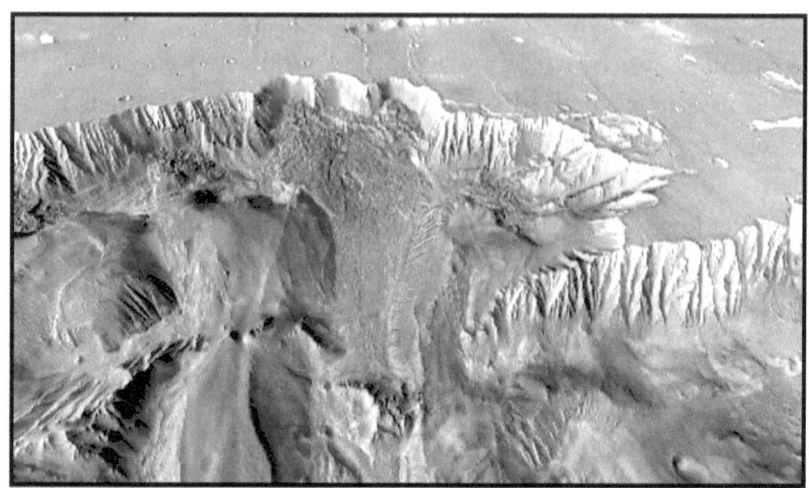

N eil Armstrong, who had recently celebrated his 90th birthday, sat on his living room couch in Lebanon, Ohio watching the CNN feed on television. As the drama of Mars 1 played out forty-five million miles away, he shook his head in amazement. It was déjà vu.

He thought back to when he and Buzz Aldrin had made their final descent to the lunar surface on *Apollo 11*. They had overshot their intended landing target, and he had been forced to take control back from the computer and fly horizontally over a huge crater full of boulders the size of cars.

He remembered every detail as if it were yesterday. The ancient computer that recycled at the rate of only once per second, flashing the overload message: *1201...1202...*The warning light that told him he had less than sixty seconds of descent fuel remaining in the tanks.

It had been a close thing.

He had once met Anna Johnson at an awards dinner. She had impressed him with her strong character and determination to succeed. They had a lot in common. Armstrong smiled to himself and took his wife's hand as they continued to watch the broadcast.

The MEV shook and roared as it continued a headfirst, full-power descent toward the Martian surface. Johnson's heart was racing like a runaway freight train. She tried not to show her anxiety as she worked. "Stand by for pitch program."

"Thirty thousand meters to ground contact," said McKendrick tersely.

As Johnson pitched the MEV around so that its landing legs were now pointed toward the surface, she felt as if her stomach had been wrenched from her body.

Walker glanced out the right-hand window, trying to gauge the terrain below. "I recognize this area. We're over the Terra Meridian."

"That's right," said Johnson. "Canyons and mountains, mostly." She resisted adding an 'I told you so.' She pressed another switch that rattled the MEV. "Shield jettison," she said. No longer needed, the red-hot heat shield that had protected the lander from heat buildup during atmospheric entry flew away from the spacecraft.

McKendrick studied the module's image on the radar screen as the MEV's descent engines screamed in the background. "Module is coming up on shield jettison. Looks like the parachutes are opening, too." In the next moment, he gasped as a tiny white blip on the radar screen suddenly blossomed to the size of a golf ball. "Look out! We're headed right for the heat shield!"

The cargo module had also jettisoned its now-useless heat shield, and the lander was descending directly into its path. A warning buzzer blared in the cabin. Johnson switched it off and reached for the manual controls to make a quick course-correction. It was too late. "Oh, my God…" She ducked away involuntarily as a huge metal panel rushed past her window and disappeared. There was a distinctive *thump* as it passed. The MEV shuddered for a moment, and then seemed to recover. Instinctively, she scanned the controls for any damage, but found nothing. "I think we clipped it," she said cautiously.

"No kidding," McKendrick said. His eyes stayed glued to the control boards. "No cautions-and-warnings, though. Cabin pressure is still holding steady."

"Damn! I just lost Houston," said Johnson. She checked the

com signal-strength meter. It read zero.

Walker tilted his head and looked out his window. From his vantage, he was able to see their com-dish. A ragged mounting pole about six inches long was all that remained of the antenna. "We've lost the X-band. K-band, too. Antenna's gone. Must have been torn away by the impact."

"26,000 meters," said McKendrick. "I'm not seeing the module on radar anymore. I think it's…" Another warning buzzer and a red light caught his attention. "Hey…we're losing fuel fast from descent tanks two and six. Looks like they're breached."

"I see it." Johnson switched off the second alarm and closed the flow valves to the damaged tanks. "They must have been struck by the heat shield, too. We'll have to dump them before they ignite." She flipped two red switches and with a pair of quick bangs, the leaking tanks flew away from the MEV.

Walker leaned over and scanned the fuel readings. "We're still within parameters on fuel for the landing. We'll have to transfer from the ascent tanks, though."

Johnson glanced at the 'abort' control for a moment. She surreptitiously moved her left hand toward it.

"24,000 meters," McKendrick said calmly. "Sixty seconds to commit point. Someone make the call."

"There's five tons of fuel in that cargo module," said Walker. "More than enough to replace any we use from the ascent tanks."

"That's not an answer." Johnson laid her left hand on the abort control. "If we can't find that module, we'll never make orbit again without more fuel. I remind you we also have no com with Houston. I think we should abort and head back to the *Lincoln* until Houston sorts this out. We can still do a full abort on the descent engines and try a landing later. We could also restore our com there."

"No!" Walker said. "No abort damn it! We stay with the module!"

"Didn't you hear me, Mike? If we abort in the next twenty seconds, we can do it without dumping the descent stage. There would still be a chance for a landing later."

"Absolutely not!" Walker said. "Divert fuel from the ascent

tanks and stay on course. That's an order."

McKendrick glared at both of them from his center couch. "Come on, you two. Make up your minds, or I'll pull that abort handle myself."

"Are we still tracking the module's homing beacon?" said Walker.

Johnson checked the homing signal and was relieved to see it was still showing. The beacon system was on a smaller, separate antenna. "Yes. I might be able to put us down within a couple of kilometers of wherever it decides to land. I can't guarantee the terrain, though."

"Do it," Walker ordered. "We'll figure out a way to restore communications after we land."

Johnson knew Walker was taking a tremendous risk by ordering a blind landing over unknown terrain. Without communications, it was beyond risky. It was a crazy gamble. However, she couldn't bring herself to override his decision. "All right. We go." She moved her hand away from the abort lever and toward another set of controls.

She was now more frightened than at any time she could remember. "Opening ascent fuel valves," she said. "Transferring fuel to descent engines." They were now burning fuel actually designated for their liftoff from the Martian surface. "There goes the reserve," she said. She increased thrust and made a slight adjustment, shadowing the module's course as it screamed toward the surface somewhere below them. She could see the fire trails from its landing engines as a long thin line.

"Estimated four minutes to touchdown," said McKendrick. "Okay that's it, guys. Twenty thousand meters to ground contact. We just passed the commit point."

At Mission Control in Houston, organized pandemonium now reigned. All communications with the MEV had died a few seconds after McKendrick had called out his warning about the cargo module's heat shield. Suddenly, Houston had lost both telemetry and radio signal.

The MEV had simply vanished.

Jim Morris stood silently at the back of the room and waited for the flight controllers to sort it out. He already suspected the worst. The heat shield on the cargo module weighed several hundred pounds. If the MEV had struck the shield, it could mean disaster. Morris tried to remain calm and keep his mind clear.

He watched as the CapCom technician frantically tried to reach the crew, calling repeatedly, "Mars One, this is Houston, do you read? Mars One, this is Houston, do you read?" There was no response.

"We've lost the radar signal on the module," said McKendrick. "Homing beacon is still there. Pretty weak signal, though."

"It may have gone into a canyon," said Johnson. "Some of them are fairly deep in this area."

At a scant two thousand meters above the ground, she increased power again to slow their descent. She saw what resembled the Grand Canyon below them, however, this place contained scores of Grand Canyons from horizon to horizon, like some colossal stone maze. They all looked dark and deep.

She spotted a few large plateaus rising above the canyons and considered putting the MEV on top of one. She decided against it. They would never reach the cargo module sitting on top of a plateau. Instead, she made another course change, flying horizontally, trying to bring the MEV closer to the module's last known position.

As they thundered over the canyons searching for a landing site, the descent engines continued to burn fuel at a furious rate.

"Watch out. I see broken terrain on radar," said McKendrick.

"Roger that." Outside her window, Johnson saw sharp-edged ridges and deep slashes across the ground that ended in shadows. "Damn, it's dark down there," she said.

It was nearly sunset on Mars. The canyons shone in dark burgundy and crimson. The light was fading fast.

She finally glimpsed something encouraging. Between two of the high plateaus was a narrow valley covered in nothing more dangerous than small rocks. It was an ancient riverbed, winding among the canyons. "I think I see a good landing site. Here we go." She leveled off and dropped them smoothly into the valley. Sheer cliffs and steep hills seemed to swallow the MEV.

McKendrick checked their fuel supply. "Sixty seconds. Open valves on tank four?"

Johnson understood the question. They had already transferred fuel from three of the six tanks on the upper ascent stage. In one minute, they would have to transfer even more if they were not on the ground. "No." She reached up to close another switch. "No transfer. Plenty of time. Landing lights on." She risked another quick glance out the window. "We're going for the riverbed," she said. "It's at least thirty meters across. No boulders. Terrain looks good."

"Radar shows same," said Walker. "Come on Anna, get it down."

Johnson watched the altimeter carefully and piloted the MEV into a gentle vertical descent, its engines still roaring and gulping fuel. As they dropped into the spot she had selected, thick rust-colored dust flew in all directions. Sensors in the landing legs brushed the ground.

"Contact light," said Johnson calmly. She flipped another switch above her head. "Engine stop."

The MEV settled to the ground with a soft bump, coming to rest at a slight angle. The engine shut down with a drawn-out whine that slowly faded into silence. The sun was completely gone now, and the darkness outside was total.

In the swirling shadows created by their landing lights and the Martian dust, they could see only tantalizing hints of the towering walls of stone surrounding the spacecraft.

Mikey

Howard Tyler entered the Mission Control room and took his usual seat in the back next to Jim Morris. "How long has it been now?"

"Four hours, thirty-two minutes since our last contact," said Morris.

"Most of the news services are saying they are probably dead. We have to make an announcement."

"How did the President sound to you?" asked Morris.

"Subdued. Sad, I suppose."

"They're not dead, Howard."

"You can't know for sure."

"I feel it."

Tyler put a comforting hand on Morris' shoulder. "You heard their last transmission, Jim. They probably struck the heat shield jettisoned from the MCM. Their velocity at that point..."

"I *know* they're alive, Howard. We're moving the Orbiter to make passes over their estimated landing site. When it's in position, we can start taking pictures and try to find them."

"Our last telemetry says they could be down anywhere within a five hundred by one thousand kilometer ellipse. It won't be easy," said Tyler.

"Look, Howard. We both know the Orbiter can resolute objects down to one meter," said Morris. "If they made it to the surface, we should be able to see them." He added, "No one is giving up on these guys."

"Neither am I, but the President still wants us to make some sort of announcement. I have a room down the hall crammed with reporters about to break our doors down. Can you handle it?"

"Give me five minutes. I'll be there in five minutes."

"Thanks."

Tyler left the room and returned to his office to meet with the senior team members from MEP. The disappointment he felt was crushing. He hoped the MEP team had something positive to say, but that was unlikely.

Morris continued watching the big screen and listening to the controller at the CapCom console. The tech kept repeating the same message. "Mars One, this is Houston, do you read…Mars One, this is Houston, do you read…"

Morris cursed and headed for the door. It was time to face the press. *What in the hell happened up there?* He thought.

All of the reporters leaped up in unison and shouted questions as Morris entered the Briefing Room. He held up a hand for silence and stepped to the podium.

"Thank you," he said. "Ladies and gentlemen, I have a short statement and then I will take your questions. At 10:38 PM Eastern Daylight Time, Mission Control lost contact with the Mars 1 crew during their final descent to the Martian surface. In their last transmission, the crew reported a problem with the heat shield on the unmanned Mars Cargo Module. Apparently, after the module jettisoned its heat shield, the MEV lander may have collided with it. All telemetry and communications with the crew ceased at that point, and we have heard nothing from them since. I want to stress that this does not mean the crew is dead, it only means that we have lost contact with them. We are moving the Mars Orbiter into a new orbit, in order to photograph the area where we think they landed."

The reporters began shouting and waving their arms again, some were actually pushing each other out of the way and throwing elbows; others were on cell phones struggling to make their initial reports. Morris stared at the reporters and put on his best professional face, wishing he were somewhere else. He knew he was going to be answering many tough questions for the remainder of the night.

Michael Walker sat on the floor of the MEV with his back against a row of storage compartments built into the wall. He stared silently out a viewing window and into the darkness. The landing lights were switched off now, in order to save power. Mars' two moons, Phobos and Deimos, shone with a pale blue-green light across the alien landscape.

Immediately after the landing, the astronauts had activated a 'contingency sample collector.' A small robot arm scooped up several pounds of rock and soil and stored them automatically in a special container mounted on the exterior of the MEV. It was supposed to ensure a piece of Mars would return to Earth in case they had to liftoff in a sudden emergency.

No one was leaving just yet. Nevertheless, mission protocol had to be followed.

Then Johnson had snapped dozens of pictures of the immediate area using a remote camera. After a complete systems check of the MEV, Walker had ordered a rest period.

The circular interior of the lander measured a scant five meters across. It was divided into two halves. The astronauts' couches and a semicircle of control boards encompassed one side. Most of the other half consisted of numerous supply compartments from floor to ceiling, with their contents listed on the front. Three windows provided excellent views, and a high-definition video camera mounted on the top of the MEV could be pointed in any direction.

A floor hatch led to the descent engine stage, where more supplies and some of the science packages were stored. The ceiling hatch had led to the Transhab, back on the *Abraham Lincoln.* That hatch would always remain closed now, since it had no airlock. A small airlock passage in the main cabin led to the only exit.

Mounted outside and underneath the MEV, and out of the way of the engine exhaust, was their small rover.

Johnson and McKendrick were sound asleep on their couches. They had snuggled into sleeping bags and dropped the couches into the reclining position. If they had wanted, they could have slept on the deck, since there was plenty of room. McKendrick was snoring lightly.

Walker could not take his eyes from the window. The light from the Martian moons cast an eerie glow among the cliffs and canyons.

Houston probably thinks we're dead, he thought. This did not concern him now. He reviewed the facts in his mind. They were safely on the surface. They could still leave anytime they wanted, once they transferred additional fuel from the module. They had a portable tracking device that would help them locate it.

A few hours ago, Johnson had gone below and dug the device out of storage. She had picked up a weak signal that gave them a rough bearing on the module. It was less than two kilometers from their landing site – somewhere. If they could reach the module and retrieve its precious supplies and fuel, they could survive on Mars for 120 days. Failing that, they had about ten or twelve days of life-support in the MEV.

Walker adjusted the sleeping bag around his shoulders and settled down onto the deck. Total exhaustion was pulling down his eyelids like a couple of lead fishing weights; he fought to keep them open. *I have to check the fuel situation. I have to stay awake.*

Less than a minute later, however, his chin dropped onto his chest and he fell into a deep sleep. He began to dream.

"Boy!"

No movement.

"Gawdamnit boy! Git your lazy ass outta that bed!"

Young Mike Walker ducked from the blow he knew would be coming, and scrambled out from under the covers in a sort of back-asswards way, scooting toward the foot of the bed. He snatched a ragged pair of jeans from the floor. He held the jeans in front of him, in a sort of defensive posture. "Yes, Pa."

"We got chores to do today," said Archie Walker. "Git dressed."

"Yes, Pa."

Pa Walker already smelled of whiskey, and it was only 6AM. Little Mikey knew it was going to be another bad day. He dressed quickly and found his shoes. He had outgrown them a few months ago. Pa had simply placed each shoe on a chopping log and cut out the leather around the toes.

Ma had gone to town earlier in the morning to do her weekly shopping at the Wal-Mart. The boy ate his meager breakfast in silence, his eyes only on his food. Pa waited over by the sink, pouring himself a shot of whiskey occasionally. "Got to hoe around the corn stalks, today," he said, slurring the words. His eyes were red.

After Mike finished his oatmeal and powdered milk, Pa led him out to the tool shed. He handed the boy a hoe, picked up one for himself, and led the way to the cornfield. "You git on over to that end," he ordered. "Work this way. Meet me in the middle." He gave the boy a hard squint and a look of warning. "Don' make me do much more'n half...or I'll tan yer hide."

"Yes, Pa."

Mike started on the first row, glad he was not working next to Pa. He chopped expertly around the base of the stalks with the hoe, cleaning out the weeds and leaving the stalks without a scratch. He moved steadily up and down the rows, working his way toward the center of the field. The morning turned into noontime, and he began to work faster. Hoeing the corn had turned into a race, with Mike the only real participant. *If I finish more than half the hoeing, Pa might stop...*he put the thought from his mind. Pa would find some excuse to belittle his work, no matter how many rows he finished. He always did.

As he reached the center of the cornfield, he stopped and listened for a minute. A soft breeze drifted though the rows.

Something was different. He realized that he hadn't heard Pa's hoe chopping through the weeds for a long time. Mike went to the end of the row and started walking along the edge of the cornfield, peering up the rows, as people do when they try to locate someone in a supermarket. *Maybe he headed back to the house for a drink.*

He saw his father lying on his back in between one of the rows. The boy approached cautiously. It was dangerous to wake Pa, especially if he was drunk.

Pa's eyes were half-open, his mouth parted slightly, and he had one hand on his chest. Mike had seen enough dead animals on the farm to know death when it visited. He reached down and touched Pa's face. It was already growing cold. He thought he should start to cry or scream, but he could not dredge those emotions to the surface.

Instead, he started for the house to tell his mother. Perhaps she had brought a treat for him from the Wal-Mart.

Someone was shaking him by his shoulders. Walker opened his eyes and looked up to see Johnson studying him with a worried look.

"Mike? You alright?"

Walker rubbed his eyes and stretched his neck back and forth until it cracked. "I'm fine. Sorry. I must have fallen asleep."

"You were moaning. It woke me up. You sure you're okay?"

Walker nodded. "I'm fine. Stress, bad dreams, I guess. Tough day at the office."

"No problem. How about if I take the watch? You should get some rest. Big day tomorrow."

Walker did not argue. He spread himself out on the deck without another word, and in a few seconds, he was asleep again.

Johnson stared at Walker for a minute or two. This was supposed to be the high point of her life, and instead it was turning into a struggle to survive.

A look of peace crossed Walker's face. She watched him dispassionately for a moment. *I can't trust him anymore,* she thought. *How the hell did NASA ever pick him for this job?* Bitterness welled up in her throat as she thought about her family, and how worried they must be right now.

Stupid bastard. I should have listened to my instincts and pulled the abort handle, or just ignored his order and gone for the short mission landing instead.

Leaving Walker, she sat down in the pilot's couch and quietly began running some additional systems checks. Her fingers flew over the controls, clicking keys and buttons like a concert pianist. A group of figures scrolled across a video screen. She saw plainly that without the stored fuel aboard the cargo module, no one was going home.

She stared at the numbers for a long time and thought about what would have happened had they simply taken the alternate landing site at Chrysse Plain.

It would have been interesting to see that old Viking lander, she thought. She looked hard at Walker, who was now snoring loudly.

Damn him. He may have killed us all.

A New World

Dawn brought views of high stone cliffs and rocky terrain, with a few thin clouds that rushed quickly across the sky. They had landed in the middle of a winding riverbed cutting between the cliffs. It was dry as a bone; the water that had carved it had vanished thousands of years ago. The sky was a pale orange and the sun a bit smaller and dimmer than on Earth. The predominant color of the ground near the MEV was rust, while veins of deep burgundy and brown painted the stone on the cliffs. The outside temperature was a relatively mild (for Mars) twenty degrees below zero, Fahrenheit. There was no wind and nothing moved around the spacecraft.

The three of them ate breakfast from ration packs and then

prepared to go outside for the first time.

Walker and Johnson waited patiently in the airlock tunnel, dressed in their EVA suits and ready to become the first humans to walk on another planet. Strangely, neither one was particularly excited about it. They had no way to tell anyone about this moment, save each other. There would be no live words spoken to a waiting world to enter into the history books.

Johnson had activated a video camera on the outside of the MEV to record the event anyway, and Walker would say something he had planned. It would be the official record. Whether anyone would ever see it was another matter entirely.

This does not feel like history, Anna thought as they waited in the airlock and made some last-minute checks of their equipment. *This is a survival situation now.* A deep resentment was building in the core of her psyche. Outwardly, she hid her feelings, but that resentment was directed at Walker.

Walker turned the airlock handle and eased the hatch outward. The cabin pressure rushed out with a loud hiss, froze into white crystal flakes, and fell to the ground. "I'm going down the ladder," he announced, backing out the door in his bulky suit.

McKendrick's calm voice came over their suit radios. "Cameras and recorders are running." His job was to monitor the MEV's systems while Johnson and Walker checked the lander for any outside damage.

Walker reached the foot of the ladder. "I'm stepping off now. There. I am on the surface. As I step onto this new world," he said slowly, "I do it in the hope that many more will follow."

McKendrick smiled. *Simple, but good,* he thought. *Easy for kids in history classes to remember later.* He watched on the video monitor as Walker bent over and picked up a small rock, examining it. He weighed it in his hand and tucked it into a pocket of his suit. He looked up and made a slashing motion across his throat. McKendrick switched off the cameras, leaving only the voice recorders running. Those never stopped.

"Okay, we did the historical bit. Now let's get to work," Walker said gruffly. He waved at Johnson to come outside and she climbed down the ladder.

The two astronauts walked completely around the MEV and examined it carefully. Except for the dish antenna, they found no obvious damage. A protective cover under the spacecraft seemed intact. Inside was the rover.

"What's the story, guys?" asked McKendrick.

"The X and K band antennas are gone," said Walker.

"Of course. Anything else?"

"Nothing visible."

"Roger that."

Johnson switched on a small device the size of a walkie-talkie. "Module tracker seems to be working," she said. "All right, I'm heading up to a high spot to get a better signal."

McKendrick acknowledged her and watched from one of the lander's three windows as Johnson made her way across the rock-strewn riverbed and toward a low hill nearby. She started climbing.

"Careful now," McKendrick warned.

"Roger that, Dale." Johnson picked her way up the hill, using some of the larger rocks as handholds. She was soon breathing heavily in the bulky EVA suit. The four months in zero gravity had sapped everyone's strength to a degree, even though all of them had exercised faithfully each day. She made the summit at last, and looked back on their landing site from a point about thirty meters above. "You should see this," she said. "It's like a maze around here. Nothing but canyons and hills."

"Anna! Can you pick up the beacon or not?" Walker asked impatiently.

"Keep your shirt on, Mike." Johnson adjusted the gain on the tracking device and extended the antenna. She moved it slowly back and forth. A green light flashed and a series of numbers scrolled across a tiny screen. She gave a thumbs-up to Walker.

"What have you got?" he said.

"Signal acquisition. Give me a second or two to lock it in."

McKendrick's voice crackled in her helmet. "Computer is ready to process your signal, Anna."

Once the computer had a fix on the location of the module, it could also provide the astronauts with detailed maps on how to reach it. Mars had been thoroughly mapped from space years ago, and this data had been loaded into the MEV computer before their launch from Earth.

Johnson triggered the device to download the homing beacon data to the MEV. "Okay. Are you receiving the beacon signal?"

"That's it," said McKendrick. "Computer has the coordinates. They're coming up on the screen now. Good job, Anna."

Johnson was already tired. She sat down on a nearby rock and scanned the general area, trying to memorize the terrain. The riverbed curved like a sidewinder snake in both directions. She saw towering hills stretching to the horizon and an orange-pink sky. A thin bit of cloud passed overhead at record speed. She had never seen a cloud move that fast across the sky. She guessed its altitude at five thousand meters.

"I think we have high-speed upper-level winds," she called. "I just saw a cloud passing by. You should have seen how fast it..."

"You're wasting O-2," Walker interrupted. "Come back down. We have a lock on the module. That's all we need right now."

"Roger that." She took a last quick glance at the vista surrounding them and then started descending the hill backwards, one cautious step at a time. It was several minutes before she reached the safety of the riverbed.

Walker was waiting at the bottom. "Are you okay?"

"I'm fine," she replied, still breathing hard from the exertion.

They climbed up the ladder to the MEV airlock and went inside. Walker pulled the hatch shut firmly and sealed it. A few seconds later, McKendrick pressurized the airlock passage and they were able to remove their helmets.

"I think I'm a little out of shape from all the time we spent in zero-g," said Johnson.

"Everyone is."

They entered the main cabin and sat down heavily with their backs against the wall. Johnson relaxed and tried to catch her breath. She looked at McKendrick. "Any data on the module?"

"It's less than two kilometers from here," McKendrick replied. "It's also sitting at the bottom of a rather deep canyon."

Walker struggled to his feet and began unzipping his EVA suit. "Are you sure?"

"Look for yourself." McKendrick entered a command for the MEV computer. Seconds later, a printer rolled out colored sheets of paper into his hand from a nearby port. "Printouts of the local area," he said, handing two of the maps to Walker. "The green dot is the module. The red dot is us."

Johnson stood up and grabbed one of the high-resolution pictures from Walker's hand. She studied it with an expert eye. "Looks like we'll have to go up this riverbed for about a thousand meters," she said, pointing to a spot on the picture. "Then we have to climb over this low ridge here. It's on the other side, in a canyon about a hundred meters down."

"We have to figure out a way to transfer the fuel, that's all," said Walker indifferently.

"Sure," said Johnson. "All we need is a magic wand to levitate those one-ton fuel canisters up to the top of that canyon, and down to where we are."

"I might know a way," said McKendrick.

"How?" asked Walker.

"We cut the module's parachute lines free," McKendrick said. "Those lines are ten thousand pound test rated. We could attach the lines to the canisters and pull them out of the canyon one at a time, using the rover. It may work if we bring them up slowly. Someone will have to go down and attach the lines, of course."

"One good bang on a rock and those high-pressure containers will blow apart like Fourth of July fireworks," said Johnson. "Forget it, Dale. It won't work. And how deep was that canyon you said?"

"About a hundred meters."

"A hundred meters? Those parachute lines are only thirty meters long. And you'd still have to get the rover up to the top of that ridge to try pulling the tanks out of the canyon. Not a chance."

"I don't have all the answers, Anna. It was just an idea." McKendrick lay back in his couch and stared at the ceiling.

"We'll unpack the rover tomorrow and take a trip up there," said Walker.

"Why not now?" asked Johnson, impatiently. "There's still about ten hours of light left."

"No. We need a plan, first. I want everyone rested up for this."

Johnson's eyes flashed. "Every minute we waste makes our chances worse, Mike. We could be up there in three hours, even counting the time it will take to unpack the rover." Adrenalin rushed through her as she stepped closer to Walker and shot him an angry stare. "Face it. You made a bad call to follow the module down anyway."

"It was my call."

"That's right. And you screwed the pooch. You went against mission parameters. Now we're stuck here, and we can't even contact Houston."

"Okay! It's all my fault. Is that what you wanted to hear?" Walker shook his head and gazed out the window. "I just don't like to lose. I wanted our four months on Mars."

"We're not getting it now, that's for sure."

"There's still a chance," Walker said. "If we can retrieve enough supplies along with the fuel in the module…"

Johnson suddenly slammed both her palms into Walker's chest, catching him by surprise. He bounced hard into the storage compartment wall. "Wake-up call, Mike!" she shouted. "We are *not* staying here for a hundred and twenty days! This is about survival now, and thanks to you, our chances are not good." She stabbed a finger toward the fuel readouts plainly visible on the controls. "Take a look at those numbers. We cannot make orbit again with that much fuel. If we somehow manage to haul those fuel containers here, we're going to transfer every drop into the MEV and go home." She turned away. "We're probably dead anyway."

"You need to calm down," Walker said.

"Why should I listen to you?" Johnson shot back. "I put up with your chauvinistic garbage for over three years just to be on this mission – and then you blow the whole thing with your stupid decisions!"

McKendrick rose from his seat and stepped between them like a referee at a boxing match. "Knock it off – *both* of you."

The ill treatment she had received over the last three years suddenly flooded to the fore. Johnson moved around McKendrick and taunted Walker in a childlike voice. "*I don't like to lose! I wanted our four months on the surface!*" She turned her back on the two men and began stripping off her EVA suit.

Walker said nothing.

McKendrick spoke. "Come on, Anna. This isn't helping."

"Okay. You were right," said Walker, "we should have gone for the short mission site as soon as we lost control of the module."

"No kidding," said Johnson. "Doing that would have kept us within the curve on the fuel. Do you realize that without being able to transfer fuel from the ascent stage, we would have crashed? That feature was added only a few months before the launch." She stepped out of the heavy EVA suit and hung it on the wall. "We have to figure out a way to get home. And our chances are not good."

"Have you run the exact numbers on our fuel, yet?"

"I know we don't have enough to make orbit. If we try a liftoff, we'll just crash back into the surface."

"Are you sure?"

"Yes. The ascent tanks are down to fifty-eight percent of capacity. The absolute minimum we need to rendezvous with the *Lincoln* is seventy-five percent. Our total fuel capacity is twenty-six tons. That means we need seventeen percent of twenty-six tons of additional fuel to make orbit. Twenty percent would be better."

"How much fuel is that?" Walker asked.

Johnson ran the problem through her head in a few seconds. "Eight thousand, eight hundred and forty pounds."

"The MCM carries five tons of fuel in one-ton tanks," said Walker. "Ten thousand pounds. We'll need…"

Johnson cut him short. "That's right, Brainiac. We need all five tanks. I hope they survived the landing."

The Storm

During the long Martian night, a soft wind began whispering through the riverbed, gently rocking the MEV from side-to-side. Everyone awoke at once and went to the windows to observe this new phenomenon. It was the first sound made by an alien planet to reach human ears. As they stared into the darkness, the soft wind changed to a hard, snapping breeze, and within minutes, it had turned into a full-blown storm. Orange dust mixed with ice crystals screamed past the windows in a surreal horizontal wall. The dust and snow made a hissing sound against the hull, like sandpaper on a board. The cabin lights in the MEV flickered, but held steady. After a few minutes, it was obvious that the storm was staying for a while.

"We're going to need a paint job when this is over," said McKendrick. He turned away from the window and climbed back into his sleeping bag on the deck, pulling the flap over his head.

"Forget it," he said. "There's nothing we can do about it. Get some rest. We've got a big day tomorrow."

Johnson continued staring out the window. "Tomorrow? Sometimes these dust storms go on for months at a time."

"Unlikely," said Walker. "In this area, the storms are more localized, and usually short-term. It shouldn't last long."

"You hope." She found her own bag on the deck and crawled into it. A moment later, she was up again and headed toward the pilot's couch, with the sleeping bag in tow. "I'll take the first watch."

Hours later, dawn broke and light returned. The storm continued raging through the riverbed valley, showing no sign of abating. Sand, pebbles, and ice crystals had pounded the tiny craft for twelve hours, and the windows were scarred with thousands of tiny scratches.

Walker opened a storage locker and passed out some breakfast rations. The three sat on the deck and ate quietly.

When they finished, Walker spoke up. "I think I've figured out a way to let Houston know we're still alive."

"How?" Johnson said.

"The surface experiments package has a seismometer, right? To detect tremors in the Mars crust?"

"Sure," said McKendrick. "It records the data and transmits it to…" His eyes grew wide as he finished the statement. "To the Mars Orbiter."

"That's right," said Walker. "And the Orbiter transmits the data back to JPL. We can set up the seismometer and strike the ground right next to it. We do it slowly, in a series, and use prime numbers."

"What about using Morse code instead, and sending them a message about our status?" asked Johnson.

"Won't work," said Walker. "The seismograph records waves in the ground. Trying to send Morse would just end up looking like a bunch of small earthquakes. No. We have to space out the strikes to the ground and take our time. One hit, then three, then five, right up the line of prime numbers. If we repeat the pattern at least five or six times, somebody at JPL may figure it out someone is trying to make contact. Just activating it will tell them we're alive, anyway."

McKendrick stretched and yawned loudly. Something in his back cracked and Johnson laughed.

"You must be getting old," she said, smiling. "That sounded bad."

"Old war wound."

"What war?"

"Rose Bowl game. I was nailed by a linebacker from the University of Washington while I was running a pass pattern across the middle. I spent the rest of the game lying on a table in the locker room."

Johnson gave him a wry look. "How do you keep passing the physicals with a back like that?"

"I don't stretch in front of the flight surgeon."

The thunderous chaos outside softened a bit and everyone fell silent to listen – and hope. A moment later, the wind gusted again to full force, slamming into the MEV with a renewed fury.

"No one's going outside in *that* stuff," said McKendrick.

"There are still a few things we can do while we wait," said Walker. He nodded to Johnson. "I want every option available to us that will save O-2 and power, including shutting down all non-essential systems. We need to know how long we can stay here, right down to the last minute."

"I can do that," she answered.

Walker looked at McKendrick. "We're going to have to dump every ounce of extra weight we can. You and I are going to start working on possibilities."

"Right." McKendrick took out a pen and a small paper tablet. He began making notes.

"Let's get to work," said Walker.

By mid-morning, Johnson had completed her calculations and systems checks. She had shut down a few unneeded systems to save power; however, she knew that power was not the real problem. *The lights will still be burning in the MEV long after we're dead*, she thought wryly. She relaxed in the pilot's couch, staring at the control boards, racking her brain for options.

The men had spent the entire morning on a different task. They had examined every square inch of the spacecraft, searching for anything that could be discarded. When they finished, they sat down to assess the results.

Johnson rubbed her eyes tiredly. "What's the verdict, guys?"

McKendrick tried to sound hopeful. "I think we can leave about twelve hundred pounds on the ground."

"You want to jettison twelve hundred pounds?" Johnson looked skeptical. "What do you have in mind...leaving an engine behind?"

McKendrick ran his hands over his face and yawned. "No. I figure we can unbolt the doors on all the storage compartments and then remove the compartments completely with the laser cutter. We can do the same to the outer airlock hatch, and a few redundant items on the hull. I have a few other ideas, too."

"No one is cutting or unbolting anything unless I check it out first," said Johnson. "You could damage a critical system and that would end our chances real quick."

"That makes sense," said Walker.

"You bet it does. For one thing, if you jettison that airlock door, atmosphere will be tearing around inside that passage during liftoff. The force could throw off our trim, flip the MEV over, and we would crash back into the surface. Did you think of that, Dale?"

McKendrick flushed red. "No. But if we *could* leave the hatch behind, it would cut payload big-time. That thing weighs a ton."

"Not that much," said Johnson.

"That was a figure of speech," said McKendrick. "But it's close to two hundred pounds I think."

"What's the story on the consumables?" asked Walker.

"Christmas," said Johnson. "Sometime around dawn on Christmas Day, we run out of O-2. The fuel cells will last another week, but that won't matter because..." She did not complete the statement, her voice trailing.

"Because we'll all be dead by then," finished Walker. He stared out the nearest window and muttered a curse at the storm raging against the little spacecraft. "Let's lower the partial pressure on the O-2 again. Maybe we can stretch out our supply a bit."

Houston

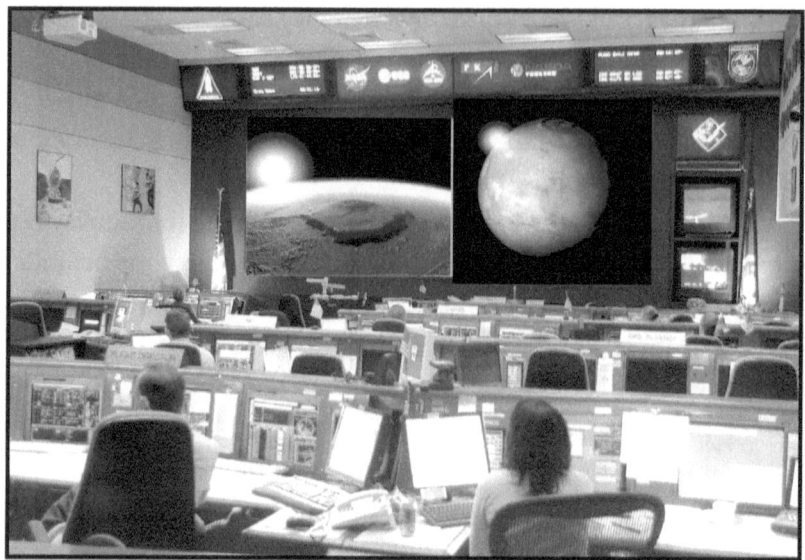

At Dr. Tyler's request, Jim Morris had reluctantly departed Mission Control in Houston and flown out to the Jet Propulsion Laboratory in Pasadena. Tyler had ordered an emergency meeting between Morris and the Mars Exploration team to discuss options. It was difficult for Morris to accept the order. He had been sleeping on a cot in his office for the past two days. The remainder of his time he had spent in the Mission Control Room, monitoring for any new developments. Morris had a strong feeling that the Mars 1 crew was still alive; however, few at NASA shared his opinion.

The final transmissions from the crew indicated the worst had happened. McKendrick's hastily shouted warning about the module's heat shield, the sudden loss of communications and telemetry, along with no further contact from the crew pointed to tragedy for the mission.

The President had already announced he would address the nation that evening.

Morris sat alone in the back row of a darkened screening room at

JPL, using a remote control to click through the latest blow-ups from the Mars Orbiter.

The meeting with the MEP team had yielded few results. Everyone agreed on two things: The Mars lander had probably collided with the shield from the cargo module, and that the fate of the astronauts was unknown. Other than that, no one agreed on anything.

Morris knew the MEP team could draw no other conclusions based on the few facts available. A thousand questions raced through his mind. *Why had Walker decided to follow the module to the surface without contacting Mission Control? If the crew had survived the landing, why hadn't they deployed the science packages or tried to make contact?*

Signals from the science experiments would tell Houston someone was alive on the surface. Nevertheless, it had been more than three days since they lost contact – and there were still no signals.

Morris clicked to the next frame in the Mars Orbiter series. This one was a photo of a very rugged area in the Terra Meridian. The picture showed only a dust storm sweeping across an area the size of Kansas. It was a mottled orange-tan patch on the screen. No surface details were visible. He clicked to the next picture.

One very slim piece of data supported Morris' gut instinct that the astronauts could be alive. If the MEV had been destroyed during the entry phase, it would have left a trail of fire, as shattered pieces screamed into the Martian atmosphere. The MEV had certainly vanished, but remote photographs taken by the *Abraham Lincoln* had revealed no evidence of a burn-up.

The images only showed the MEV and the cargo module meeting in space, then the cargo module beginning its run for the surface, with the MEV following. There was no flash, no explosions, or fire in any of the pictures.

We would have seen something, Morris thought. He knew there were so many possibilities. It was frustrating to think about it. He clicked to another picture. It was a photograph of the same area, and of the same dust storm. He stared hard at the screen.

A thought popped into his mind. He took out his cell phone.

Andy Collins, the young scientist from Cal-Tech who had originally proposed the Mars mission plan, answered the call. "Yeah," he mumbled.

"This is Jim Morris. How are you?"

"Fine, sir." Collins sounded very tired.

"I'm in the JPL screening room. Have you seen the latest images from the Orbiter?"

"Yes. They download directly to my computer. My team has been over them with every known enhancement program."

"Find anything new?"

"Not yet."

"That dust storm over the Terra Meridian," said Morris. "Do we know when it started?"

"I can find out, sir. Hold on."

Morris heard typing on a computer keyboard, a pause, and then more typing.

"Okay," said Collins. "The storm appeared about twenty-two hours after we lost contact. Does this mean something I should know about?"

"Mission Control thinks that the cargo module was headed for a landing in that area."

"Excuse me, sir, but we already know that," Collins said. "If you have something new…"

"It's just a theory. I was thinking that the crew wouldn't be able to set up the science packages in a dust storm," explained Morris, "which could explain we haven't heard from them. I've been climbing into their shoes and trying to figure out what they would do, assuming they landed safely."

"Maybe they decided to try and locate the module first, before doing anything else," said Collins. "Or if they landed in the Terra Meridian then perhaps the storm hit before they could deploy the packages." He added, "This is all based on the idea that they are still alive after colliding with the heat shield."

"I know."

"Do you think they're still alive?" Collins asked quietly.

"There's a chance. What do you think?"

"It's possible. However, a landing in the Terra Meridian would have required a lot of fuel. All our simulations show that the MEV would have had to transfer substantial fuel from their ascent tanks in order to do it. They could be sitting on the ground right now and short on fuel. I studied the transcript of their last transmissions. Walker gave an order to chase the module to the surface. We know the module landed in the Terra Meridian. So it's possible that if the impact from the heat shield didn't take them out, they tried a landing in the same area."

"Yes," said Morris, "we're still receiving a homing signal from the module. It's weak, but we have pinpointed its location."

"You've seen maps of the Terra Meridian," said Collins. "Not the best place for radio signals."

"As if it were sitting in a canyon," said Morris.

"Very likely. Or a deep crater."

"Any ideas?"

"Keep monitoring for signals from the science packages," said Collins. "The crew might try to activate them when the dust storm lifts, assuming they are alive and even in that area."

"We're doing that already. Anything else?"

"Pray."

"I've been doing my share of praying. Thanks." Morris ended the call. He flipped to another Mars photograph with the remote and studied it for the tenth time.

As scheduled, Graham Richardson went on television at six p.m. from the Oval Office. He looked exhausted, and his shoulders were hunched over as he spoke.

"My fellow Americans," he said, "and to those of you watching from around the world, it is with a heavy heart that I address you this evening." He took a sip of water to clear his throat before he continued.

"Three and a half days ago, we lost contact with the Mars 1 crew as they were attempting to land on the surface of Mars. I can assure you that NASA is making every possible effort to locate Michael

Walker, Dale McKendrick, and Anna Johnson."

Richardson fought to control his emotions, swallowed hard, and looked directly into the television cameras. "NASA officials have also informed me that the MEV spacecraft has only enough oxygen to last the crew until sometime early morning, Eastern daylight time, Christmas Day."

As the speech continued, reporters around the globe, realizing this was the first announcement about how long the crew could actually survive without the supply module, scrambled to file updates.

In minutes, headlines popped up all over the internet. CHRISTMAS LAST CHANCE FOR ASTRONAUTS, the New York Times would shout in bold letters the next morning. CNN was already doing 24-hour coverage on the mission, parading different experts who espoused their theories on the possible fate of the crew and their chances of survival. Most were negative.

Richardson spoke for another fifteen minutes on subjects such as courage, hope, and America's continued presence in space. His words sounded sad and hollow. When the broadcast was over, he shook hands with the TV crew and exited through a side door. As he headed off to attend a special NASA briefing, he said a silent prayer. *Hey, God. How about a little Christmas miracle?*

December 19

The sudden silence woke Anna Johnson from her fitful sleep. She was dozing in the pilot's couch, wrapped in her sleeping bag. She had been tossing all night as the storm continued to rage outside the MEV. Now it was quiet, and she lifted her head in curiosity. The storm was gone. It was still dark outside, and with the lights inside the spacecraft turned off to save power, she could barely discern the forms of Walker and McKendrick sleeping on the floor.

She lay back quietly and relaxed. For five long days, they had endured the howling of the Martian winds, eating cold meals, and discussing options. It was as if Mars was protesting their presence on the planet, and Mars had certainly made its complaints known.

She knew their chances of survival were not good. On the other hand, she was eager to work on a plan, any plan, to get home. *I may have to push these guys along a bit*, she thought. She had discovered more about her male counterparts in the last five days than she had in the three years they had worked together. She closed her eyes and went back to sleep.

Light began to pour through the scarred windows on the MEV as sunrise peeked over the canyon rims. Johnson rubbed her eyes and yawned. She pushed off the sleeping bag and checked some readouts on the control boards. The environmental indicators confirmed that the storm had indeed passed. She activated the outside TV camera, which had been retracted to protect it from damage. She panned the camera using a tiny joystick control and studied the images on a small video screen. Rock walls in layered colors of dark red and brown, the riverbed, and some surrounding hills appeared. She began recording the images digitally for storage. *Someone has to see this,* she thought. *It's beautiful.*

"What are you doing?" said Walker. He cocked his head in surprise. "Hey, when did the storm let up?"

Johnson glanced down at him. He was propped up on his elbows. "About an hour ago," she said. "It's sunrise. I'm checking the area with the remote cam."

"How does it look?"

"Wind speed is negligible. Outside temperature is fifteen below zero, clear skies. Usual weather on Mars."

McKendrick stirred. He was awake in seconds, sitting up quickly. "What's new?"

"Storm's passed," said Johnson.

"Time to go to work then," he said, rolling out of his bag. He headed into the airlock to use the toilet.

Walker scratched at his stubbly beard. "I've been thinking."

"Dangerous prospect," said Johnson. She turned her attention back to the video screen.

"Hey, I already said I made a bad call to follow the module down. What the hell else do you want from me?"

"Let's get something straight," said Johnson, "I don't trust you anymore. I had to work twice as hard just to get here, because you didn't want a female on the crew. After all that, you made a decision that puts both the mission and our lives in jeopardy. I wouldn't trust you to lead me around the block, let alone figure out a way for us to get home."

Walker took the seat next to her. "Okay. From now on, we make the decisions together. All three of us. How's that?"

McKendrick emerged from the airlock passage with a pensive expression. "I could hear you guys. What's the problem now?"

"Nothing," said Walker, "no problem."

"Oh, I think there's a problem, all right." Johnson said.

"This can't be good." McKendrick opened one particular storage compartment on the wall. Reaching inside, he pulled out three plastic containers the size of cigar boxes. He dropped one each into the laps of Johnson and Walker. He kept one for himself. "Breakfast time." McKendrick made a show of reading the contents of his own box. "Reconstituted bacon-type protein strips, biscuits, black coffee, Tang, easy-open dried fruit, and condiments. Good one." He shook his head. "You two need to lighten up. We're not dead yet." He sat down on his sleeping bag and started exploring his breakfast.

After a few quiet moments, Walker and Johnson stopped glaring at each other and followed his example. As they ate, the mood inside the cramped confines of the MEV eased a bit.

The wheels never stopped rolling in McKendrick's brain. He had studied the picture carefully that showed the location of the cargo module. The module was sitting in a narrow canyon about a hundred meters down a very steep slope. *I have to figure out another option,* he thought. *No way can we pull those fuel tanks out of a hole that deep.* "Hey," he said between bites. "I have an idea on how to get that fuel."

Walker glanced up in interest. "Let's hear it."

"We could fly the MEV to the module."

Johnson spoke through a mouthful of biscuit. "I've already

thought of that. Too much fuel. We'd use too much fuel."

"Have you run the numbers on it?" Walker piped up.

She gulped down a biscuit. "No. But, we'd have to burn fifteen hundred pounds, at least."

"That much?" said McKendrick.

"Probably closer to a ton."

"You said we needed how much fuel to make orbit?"

Johnson sipped her coffee. "Eight thousand eight hundred and forty pounds additional. Absolute minimum. There is only ten thousand pounds on the module, assuming none of the canisters are damaged." She did a rough calculation in her head. "We'd still be almost a thousand pounds short after moving the MEV, and that's assuming we can actually transfer all the stored fuel to the MEV."

"I still think we might be able to haul the canisters out of the canyon," said Walker. "Maybe we can use the laser cutter and construct some type of sled to haul them out with, so they don't hit rocks."

Johnson laughed. "Not a chance, Mike."

McKendrick took out his satellite photograph and handed it to Walker. "Take a good look, Mike. See those canyon walls? It's about a hundred meters to the bottom, straight down. You're talking about hauling the canisters out of there by using some parachute lines and the rover. It just can't be done."

"We're going up there today to check it out," said Walker. "Then we'll know what can't be done."

An hour later, the three of them got into their EVA suits and prepared for the expedition to the module. Everyone checked everyone else. When Walker was satisfied, he led them through the outer hatch and down the ladder to the surface. Their plan for the day was simple. First, they would unload the science packages from a storage area under the legs of the MEV. After setting up the different instruments, they would lower the rover vehicle to the ground. The rover was barely larger than a golf cart, and although it was designed to carry only two people, all three of them would crowd into it for the trip up the riverbed.

Walker bent over and pulled hard on a gold-braided lanyard hanging under the MEV. A large square door on the belly of the spacecraft swung open. He leaned over and stuck his head up through the opening. He saw at once that most of the equipment inside was damaged. The impact from the module's shield had shattered their delicate parts. Walker found one item still attached to the deck and used his wire cutters to free it. He ducked out of the opening and handed the tiny machine to McKendrick. "Seismometer," he said.

McKendrick gave him a thumbs-up and moved the device carefully away from the MEV.

"That's it," said Walker, closing up the storage hatch. "Looks like everything else in there is junk. Set that seismometer up and see if it still works. I'll start unloading the rover."

"Right," McKendrick replied. He and Johnson carried the instrument package to a flat spot on the riverbed about twenty meters distant. The seismometer was the size of a loaf of bread with a small dish antenna mounted on top. Setup was mostly automatic. McKendrick pressed a couple of small buttons on its side. A light flashed on, telling him that it was functional and now activated. Any quakes, tremors, even the footfalls of the astronauts, would be relayed to the Mars Orbiter for transmission back to Earth – if it worked.

None of them thought of the seismometer as an experiment anymore. It was strictly a crude communications device now, and the only way to tell anyone listening they were still alive.

Open Rebellion

As Walker finished checking out the rover, Johnson was busy unloading spare oxygen tanks from a storage compartment on the side of the MEV. It was difficult work in her bulky suit, but she managed to pull six of them free. She carried each one to the rover and stacked them upright inside a metal box that was originally designed to carry rock samples. When she finished securing the tanks, she tapped Walker's shoulder. "We're ready."

"Good."

"Rover systems check out fine," announced McKendrick from the passenger seat. "Batteries are fully charged."

Walker climbed behind the wheel of the rover. "Let's move, then." The other two crowded into the other single seat.

Walker shifted into low gear and touched the accelerator. With a soft crunch on the river gravel and a sharp hum, the small vehicle began rolling forward at three kilometers per hour. Its six wheels moved up and down as it bumped along the dry riverbed and over the scattered rock.

Johnson kept an eye on the tracking monitor she carried. They were moving toward the cargo module, that much was certain. Being able to find it was another.

After a few minutes, she pointed up ahead. "It's about a thousand meters in front of us, and to the right."

The riverbed was bumpy and rough. Johnson, riding between the two men, had to keep reaching up for a handhold bar. McKendrick had a tight grip on a side rail. Walker guided the rover along as cautiously as he could.

"Wish we had time to pick up a few rocks," said McKendrick. He drank in the alien landscape with a keen eye, making mental notes. "There's a lot of unique strata around here. It's a good geological record. We need samples."

"Later," replied Walker. "Maybe."

"Should be up around the next bend," said Johnson.

Walker finally saw the ridge that McKendrick had shown them earlier on the map. The hill was nearly vertical, and covered in loose rock. It ended in a razor-sharp summit. He switched off the electric motor and stared in awe at the barrier they faced. He got out and walked toward the base of the hill. McKendrick and Johnson followed.

Walker tried to imagine climbing up that ridge. He saw himself sliding right back down and perhaps puncturing his suit or cracking his faceplate. "We'll need some rope to get up there. We have some core sample pipes we can pound into the ground for stakes, maybe use them as pitons."

"What rope?" said McKendrick. "There's nothing on the MEV."

"We can blow the emergency parachutes and cut the nylon lines. We'll tie them together, set the core pipes with a hammer, and then run a line all the way to the top."

"If we blow the parachute cover, the hatch could drop straight back down on the MEV and damage the hull," said Johnson. "Too dangerous."

"How can we get to those parachutes, then?" Walker asked.

"Remove the cover manually. And be real careful around those explosive bolts when you do."

"Sounds reasonable," said McKendrick. "We'll save at least three hundred pounds of payload by getting rid of the cover and the 'chutes, anyway."

"An added bonus," said Johnson.

"All right," said Walker. He checked a tiny readout screen on his wrist. "We have another sixty minutes of O-2. Let's take a quick look around before we head back." He started walking along the base of the hill. The other two followed.

McKendrick bent over and picked up a small blue rock that caught his eye, studying it as he walked. "There's hematite here. Clear evidence of past water. This really *was* a river flowing through here at some point in time." He tucked the rock into a pocket of his suit.

"Look," said Walker, pointing. "There's a cave up there. See it?"

Just ahead of them, a dark hole in the rock beckoned like a giant black mouth. The stone around the mouth was worn smooth from the Martian winds. They stood at the entrance and tried to see into the darkness beyond the opening, without success.

Walker switched on his helmet lights. "You two stay here," he said. "I'm going in to check this out. Maybe it goes through to the other side."

"Don't go too far," said Johnson.

"I won't. Give me ten minutes."

McKendrick and Johnson watched apprehensively as Walker disappeared into the cave. His lights flashed patterns of color on the walls for a few seconds, and then he was gone.

"Mike," called McKendrick on his suit radio.

"I hear you. This thing is big. It opens up into the size of a subway tunnel. I can see light coming from the other end. I think it goes through to the other side. I'm going to look. Stand by."

"Roger that. Be careful."

"Don't worry, I will."

"Roger."

Walker checked each of his steps in advance with a cautiously outstretched foot as he went deeper into the cave. A pinpoint of light in the far distance beckoned him forward. He headed toward it. The light grew larger as he approached and he picked up the pace a bit. Static in his helmet told him that the cave was now smothering his radio signal, but he didn't care. He had to see what was beyond the light.

He pulled out a flashlight from his suit and switched it on, checking for obstructions or danger. He saw nothing except a high-ceilinged tunnel that looked amazingly uniform in height and width. *This planet is probably full of secrets,* he thought, his heart beating faster. The exit light grew larger, and he moved even more quickly, eager to see whatever lay on the far side. As he reached the end of the tunnel, he shaded his eyes and stepped out warily into daylight.

The satellite photo generated by the MEV's computer had been right. He found himself standing on a small ledge outside the cave-tunnel. A path along the steep drop led away to the left and right, but it was far too narrow to negotiate in a bulky pressure suit. He got down on one knee and peered over the edge into the canyon. The canyon walls rose above him on all sides. He counted dozens of multicolored layers in the walls.

At the bottom of the canyon, draped in orange parachutes and tangled white nylon lines, sat the cargo module. The automatic guidance system had managed to land it on a flat spot that was barely wider than the module itself. It looked undamaged, although it was covered with orange dust from the storm. It sat on four stubby legs, a strobe light on its roof flashing at regular intervals.

Installed in each astronaut's helmet was a tiny video camera. He reached up and switched his on, recording the scene below. He moved his head gently from side to side, panning the general area. When he was satisfied he had obtained enough good images, he turned and headed back into the tunnel.

He emerged on the other side a few minutes later and gave the other two a thumbs-up. "I found the module. It looks intact."

"This cave's a passage across to that canyon?" asked McKendrick.

"Yes." Walker tapped on the top of his helmet. "I have it all on video, too. There's nothing more we can do here right now. It's about a twenty-meter drop from the end of the cave to the bottom of the canyon. We'll need some rope to get down there." He started back to the rover. "Come on. Let's get back."

Half an hour later, they were back inside the relative safety of the lander and pulled off their helmets. Walker attached a USB cable to the camera on his own helmet and connected it to a special port on the control panels. "We'll run the video I made and see if..."

Johnson interrupted him quietly. "I don't care about your damn video right now," she said. She took a seat in the pilot's couch and started typing something on the MEV computer.

"What are you doing?" Walker said.

She made a few more strokes on the keyboard and pressed the enter key. "I just coded all the ignition controls to a password."

"What for?"

"Because I'm taking command, that's why."

Walker's face scrunched up and flushed red with anger. He grabbed her arm and jerked her roughly from the couch. "Like hell you are!"

"You stupid son-of-a-bitch!" She doubled up her fists and scrambled to her feet. "No one pushes me around like that, especially some chauvinistic piece of crap like you!"

As the two lunged at each other like a couple of wolves ready to rip each other to pieces, McKendrick stepped in and pushed them apart. "Knock it off, you two! Now!"

Johnson and Walker stared at each other with hatred in their eyes, breathing hard.

"You went against mission parameters," said Johnson, leaning around the taller McKendrick and thrusting an angry finger at Walker. "Look where we are now. We don't have a snowball's chance in hell of transporting those canisters back here. So stop spouting that stupid idea. It won't work! I'm not taking any more orders from you."

"I made a mistake," said Walker. "I admitted that. But that doesn't mean you suddenly get to take command."

"Then why don't you just make it easier and turn command over to me right now," said Johnson.

"Not a chance," said Walker. His eyes bored calmly into hers. "Besides, you're the number three, remember? Dale's second-in-command. Not you."

The tension in the confined space was thick as miner's coffee.

"All right," Johnson looked to McKendrick. "How about it,

Dale? You up to the job?" She practically spat out her next words. "I'm not taking any more orders from him."

McKendrick looked at Walker as if he were asking for permission to mutiny.

"Don't look at him!" She smacked McKendrick's chest sharply with her hand. "This is between you and me, not him. *You* decide."

"I don't know, Anna. This can only make things worse."

"You want Mike to keep giving the orders? You think we should listen to *him* and spend what little time we have left trying to drag those fuel containers out of that canyon?" She threw up her hands. "It's a waste of time and oxygen, and if even one of them springs a leak or explodes, we'll never get off this rock!"

Instead of answering her, McKendrick turned to Walker. "I think she's right. We don't have any choice. We have to move the lander to the module and then see our options."

"I didn't say I thought we should move the lander," said Johnson. "It would use too much fuel to do that, remember?"

"New plan," said McKendrick. "I say we try dumping weight first, and then run the fuel numbers again. If we can jettison enough extra weight, we might be able to do it."

Johnson went to the storage compartments and retrieved something from one of them. "I need some coffee." As she did, she heard a familiar sound and uttered a curse.

McKendrick went to the nearest window and squinted through the scratched glass. "Damn it. I think the storm's coming back."

The wind had already picked up noticeably and was starting to howl through the canyon. Within seconds, the howling escalated to a terrible roar and the MEV began to rock slowly back and forth.

Johnson forgot about the coffee and slumped down against the nearest wall. She hung her head and put her face into her hands. She didn't have to run the numbers again on the fuel situation. She already knew their options, and none of them spelled survival.

It's hopeless, she thought. Tears trickled between her fingers. She kept them hidden from the two men until the tears stopped, and then got up to finish making the coffee.

Lighten the Load

As darkness fell, they began stripping out and discarding storage compartments, science packages, and anything not nailed down or necessary. Walker was busy in the airlock passageway unbolting some handrails and a light fixture. He was still in his EVA suit, and had opened the outer hatch. Each time he successfully removed a bit of unneeded hardware, he tossed it out through the door.

McKendrick was doing the same thing in the main cabin, carefully searching out and gathering cover panels, storage compartments, and their extra gear. Hand tools from a small kit were strewn haphazardly across the deck. He stacked the panels and the other items near the inner airlock door for disposal. He called Walker on the intercom. "Mike?"

"Go ahead."

"I've got a lot of stuff piled up here. Ready to jettison it?"

"Okay," Walker looked up to the small inset window in the door and gave him a thumbs-up. "I'm sealing the door." He pulled the outer hatch closed and locked it. "Go ahead and repress."

McKendrick leaned across Johnson, who was running numbers on the fuel again from the pilot's couch. "Airlock repress," he said, flipping one certain switch.

"More wasted oxygen," she said.

"It's necessary," replied McKendrick.

Compressed air rushed into the passageway. A green light flashed on the control panels. McKendrick went to the inner door and opened it. He and Walker started picking up the unneeded items and moving them carefully into the airlock. When they finished, there was hardly room for Walker to move around in the passage. McKendrick shut the inner hatch.

Walker opened the outer hatch again and threw the panels, gear, and the storage compartments outside. Fortunately, the heavy wind was coming from the opposite side of the MEV, and the open airlock was partially sheltered from the storm. In the lower gravity of Mars, he was able to toss the assorted gear a bit farther than on Earth. He tried to scatter it around, and not create a messy pile near the lander itself. After he had completed the task, he sealed the hatch once more. "That was at least three hundred pounds. Looks like a junkyard out there," he called over his suit radio. "Hope we didn't toss out the brakes and the steering wheel, too."

"Don't worry," McKendrick answered. "I had Anna check it all first. She approved."

Walker had no comment. "Okay, that's everything. I'm coming back inside."

McKendrick repressurized the airlock one more time, and then pulled the door open for Walker.

Walker removed his helmet and took a deep breath. "Lot of work," he said. Sweat was running down his face in rivulets. Once he was free of his bulky EVA suit, he hung it on the wall. "Anything new on those fuel numbers?"

"Some," said Johnson. "I had Dale weigh every piece of gear on the rock scale, and then throw that away, too. We've jettisoned about three hundred and fifty pounds so far. I ran the fuel numbers based on that. We're getting close to being able to move the MEV into the canyon without using too much fuel, but we'll have to ditch another nine hundred pounds of payload before we try a liftoff to orbit. And that's assuming we can access all the additional fuel on the module."

"Nine hundred?" Walker was incredulous. "How in the hell are we going to do that?"

"I figure we can get three hundred of it from the parachutes and the access cover," said Johnson, "and probably another two hundred or so from the outside video array and a few other items. Just before we lift off, we can also jettison whatever food and water we have left."

"Well, that adds up to five hundred pounds with another four hundred to go," said Walker. "Extra food and water won't even come close to four hundred pounds. I hope you have some other ideas."

"I'm working on it."

"You'll think of something," said Walker.

"Another thing – I checked on the parachutes. We can't unbolt the cover; it's not designed for that. We'll have to blow the hatch."

"I thought you said it was too dangerous."

"You didn't leave us too many options by parking us here, you know. I'm doing the best I can, no thanks to you."

McKendrick looked up from his work and tried to derail another possible fight. "Take it easy, guys. We're sitting at a slight angle. The cover should land some distance away after it blows. Hey, I'm hungry. Anybody else want to eat?"

"All you think about is food," said Johnson.

"We have to dump it all anyway," said McKendrick.

Walker nodded. "Do we have any more ham meals?"

The food packages had been tossed on the floor, since McKendrick had removed all the doors to the storage compartments earlier. He dug through the pile of plastic packages and tossed one to Walker. "Ham it is. How about you, Anna?"

She kept working. "You eat. I'm busy."

McKendrick walked up to stare over her shoulder. He saw immediately that she was calculating angles, thrust, and numbers for a liftoff burn. "You've got something?" he asked quietly.

"Something we haven't discussed."

"What now?"

Johnson rubbed her neck and stretched. "There's another option we might have to face to save weight. I think we all know what it is."

"No one is staying behind," said McKendrick. "We'll just have to lighten the load a bit more. In the morning, we start cutting out the storage compartments. I have other ideas, too."

"I'm sure you do," Johnson said. "But if we can't get the weight down enough..."

"We're not leaving anyone behind," McKendrick said firmly. "We'll find a solution."

"Right. If you say so."

The dust storm continued pounding the MEV, hissing and wailing through the canyon like a banshee. The lights flickered occasionally.

Johnson, still sitting in the pilot's couch, flipped a series of switches above her head. "I'm cutting the power load on the fuel cells. We need the cabin heaters a lot more than lights." As the overhead lights faded out and the MEV cabin was thrown into darkness, everyone seemed to unwind a bit. A soft glow from the control panels and a few blinking lights were the only illumination.

"We lost the seismograph transmission about an hour ago," said Johnson in a subdued tone. "The storm took it out. It did relay signals for a few minutes, though. Maybe some got through to JPL."

"They wouldn't," said McKendrick. "Unless NASA moved the Orbiter. Our present position puts us out of range. The seismograph signals can't reach the Orbiter from here."

"Not necessarily," said Walker. "They may still have the signal from the module, right?"

"Did we get off the transmission about following the module to the surface before we lost the antenna?" McKendrick said.

"I think so," said Johnson. "Yes...I think we did."

McKendrick found his sleeping bag and laid it out on the deck. Unzipping his coveralls, he stripped down to his underwear and climbed into the bag, pulling it up over his head. "We may as well relax," he said in a muffled voice from inside the bag. "If we make it back to the *Lincoln*, we can call JPL ourselves and find out if they got the signal. Otherwise, the point is moot. They can't help us now. I'm getting some rest. I suggest you do the same." Within seconds, he was fast asleep.

"That man can sleep anywhere," said Walker.

"Are you kidding? I watched him fall asleep in a tube tent a few thousand feet below the summit on Mount McKinley. The wind was whipping his tent at fifty or sixty knots." She chuckled. "I wonder how he does in a real bed."

"The same, probably."

After a few quiet seconds, Johnson spoke. "Hey, Mike."

"Yes."

"I want to apologize for losing my temper earlier."

"Forget about it. We've all been under a lot of stress."

"No, I mean it. I always figured you were against me since we started training for the mission. I resented it."

"It's no secret I was against your assignment," said Walker. "I knew this mission was a big gamble from the start. I just thought three men would have a better chance for success. Guess I was wrong. You've pulled your weight this entire trip, and more."

"Thanks."

"You know, Dale was right about something today."

"What's that?"

"If we don't start getting along and working together, our chances are less than zero of making it home."

"It's hard for me to trust you, Mike. Try to understand. You played with our lives."

"Fine. I screwed up. And if one of us has to call this place home for good, then I'll be the one who stays behind. In the meantime, I need you to keep working the numbers on the fuel. Pull up all the engineering specs and see if there is anything more we can jettison even if it means creating some calculated risks. I don't care if it's an extra screw in a cover panel."

"Remember what I said about dumping the airlock door?"

"Sure. You said it would throw off our trim at liftoff."

"I think I can work through it. It means a manual liftoff and no navi-computer until we reach orbit. However, if we toss out all the floor plating in the airlock and cut off the door, we can drop another three, maybe four hundred pounds of payload."

"Do you think you can handle a liftoff like that? You were right about the trim problem. Atmosphere rushing into the passageway is going to throw this bird around like a bouncing ping-pong ball."

"We don't have a choice."

"That's not what I asked. I asked if you could handle it."

McKendrick stirred in his bag. "Knock it off, you two. I'm trying to sleep here."

Johnson ignored the remark. "Yes, I can handle it."

"Okay. If we need to do it, the outer hatch goes, and anything else in that airlock we can safely ditch. Good enough?"

"Good enough."

"How about getting some sleep now?"

"One more thing."

"What's that?"

"Hand me one of those food packs? I haven't eaten all day."

Walker found one from the pile on the deck and tossed it to her. "Thanks."

The hissing of dust and sand rushing through the riverbed canyon was strangely soothing. Johnson finished her little meal and then tucked her sleeping bag tighter, settling into the couch. The tension of the last few days was suddenly forgotten. In a couple of minutes, she was asleep.

Signs of Life

The Jet Propulsion Laboratory
Pasadena, California
U.S.A.

When Graham Richardson had taken the bold step of committing a manned mission to Mars, American pride had quickly risen to an all-time high. The Mars 1 mission had captured the imagination of the entire world.

However, in the space of a few brief seconds, the Cinderella story had ended with a voice shouting out a sudden warning – and then nothing. McKendrick's last radio transmission had been played in the media constantly for the last week. The fate of the astronauts was on everyone's mind. Everybody had a guess or an opinion. People talked about it at work, or they tuned in at home for new developments.

Unfortunately, all the press could do was repackage the original information from NASA. There had been no new developments, and no sightings from the Mars Orbiter photos. CNN was still doing twenty-four hour coverage; but the television announcers were beginning to feel the exhaustion of recycling the same old news.

The remainder of the networks had finally resumed their normal programming, with occasional updates. CNN doggedly presented new angles on the same story, as well as interviewing experts from every field of space science. Nevertheless, as each day passed without news, even CNN was considering a cutback in coverage. Hope was dwindling.

Winter was making its presence felt, as well. A heavy storm

dumped a big load of snow on the East Coast from Maine to Virginia. More was expected in the next ten days. Boston, New York, and Washington, D.C. had suffered the worst, experiencing rolling blackouts due to exploding transformers. An icy rain swept down from the Arctic and coated everything with clear ice. One quarter of the trees in greater Boston had frozen and split, or simply collapsed to the ground from the sheer weight of the ice.

In New York City, the streets were still plowed each day, but the parking meters remained buried in snowdrifts four feet high. Thousands of cars were entombed along with the meters.

Everyone began to prepare for a different kind of holiday season. This particular Christmas, unlike any one previously, was to be a national day of mourning for three astronauts.

Andy Collins was sleeping on the couch in his apartment in Pasadena. He was dressed in slacks and a blue shirt, the same clothes he had worn for three straight days. Other staff at JPL had finally forced him to go home and get some rest. He left his car in the parking lot and took a cab. Sheer exhaustion made him a danger to be on the road, and he was smart enough to realize it.

Scarcely had he locked the door behind him and slipped off his shoes when he collapsed onto the couch. He was asleep before his head hit one of the little decorator pillows.

Some time later, the persistent ringing of the telephone woke him, grudgingly. Collins reached for his glasses and pushed them onto his face. He picked up the phone and checked the caller ID before answering. "Yeah?"

"You sound like you're still in bed." It was Kimberly Mason, one of his research assistants. "Do you know what time it is?"

"No," growled Collins.

"It's three in the afternoon."

Collins rubbed his head and yawned. "Okay, I overslept. I've been working for almost three days straight. Did you call me to tell me what time it is, or do you have something new?"

"We may have a signal from the crew. You need to check the

data on this and see what you think."

Suddenly, Collins was sitting upright and fully awake, adrenalin shooting through his veins like a high-pressure fire hose. "What have you got?"

"We have a transmission from one of the MEV's science packages."

"What? Which one?"

"The seismometer."

"That figures. Is it still transmitting?" Collins was already heading toward the kitchen to make coffee. He pinched the telephone between his shoulder and ear and filled a carafe with some bottled water.

"No. We picked up about twelve minutes of data from the seismometer, and then it stopped. The signal has not returned."

"I'll be there in half an hour," said Collins. He hung up and opened the cupboard to find the coffee. The big can was empty. He left it on the counter and dashed into the bathroom to change clothes. There was enough free coffee available at JPL right now to fill a swimming pool.

An hour later, Collins, Kimberly Mason, and one of the designers of the seismograph science package were crowded around a computer screen in the MEP offices at JPL.

The designer pointed to a series of squiggly lines portrayed against a white background. "That's it, twelve, maybe thirteen minutes of transmission," he said.

"Where did it originate?" said Collins.

"It was too short a signal to triangulate exactly. We've narrowed it down to an area in the Terra Meridian."

"That makes sense," said Collins, "we know the cargo module landed there."

"It doesn't prove a thing," said Mason. "If the MEV crashed, the science packages may have been scattered in the wreckage. It could have activated the seismometer accidentally for a few minutes."

Collins shook his head firmly. "I don't think so. I called Jim Morris on the way here to ask his opinion. He says the storage container for the seismometer is extremely rugged and fastened very securely. Any force strong enough to rip it from the storage compartment on the lander would have destroyed it. He was absolutely sure on that point."

"But there's the storm factor to consider," said the designer.

"You're talking about the dust storm over the Terra Meridian," said Collins. "What's that have to do with it?"

"The storm broke yesterday for a few hours," he explained. "The transmission started two hours later. When the Mars Orbiter passed over the Terra Meridian, it picked up homing signals from the cargo module, and then thirteen minutes of transmissions from the seismometer. I'm telling you, Andy...this is human activity. Someone on Mars is still alive."

"They might be alive," said Collins, "but not for much longer."

"What do you mean?"

"If they were able to lift off, they would have done it already. They obviously have a problem. It could be the fuel."

Graham Richardson sat alone at his desk in the Oval Office, reading the updated report about the seismograph signals picked up by JPL. When he finished reading the report, he placed it reverently into a drawer. *I'll have to address the nation on Christmas morning,* he thought. *They'll expect it.*

NASA was keeping a tight lid on the news about the seismograph signal. The final decision whether or not to release the information publicly had been dropped directly in the President's lap. Richardson considered the consequences. A part of him wanted to tell the press about the signal, another part of him said no. It would create false hope. All the evidence pointed toward two possibilities: Either the crew was already dead, or they would die from lack of oxygen come Christmas morning. Due to the seismograph signals, the second possibility was now much more likely. The astronauts had made it to Mars, but they couldn't leave.

For the first time since he had taken office, he had no clear idea what to do. *Should I tell the families of the astronauts this new information?* He took a small sip of coffee. A feeling of serenity passed through him, like a slow-moving river patiently winding its way toward the ocean. When he asked himself what the crew would have wanted, the answer popped into his mind. They would want their loved ones to know they had reached Mars alive, even if they couldn't come home.

Richardson picked up the telephone to call the families of the astronauts.

Three thousand miles away, and in a city with much better weather, Jim Morris and the Mars Exploration team were gathered in the same room at JPL where they had first discussed a possible Mars mission three and a half years ago. This meeting was different. Most in attendance had long faces or looked depressed.

Morris entered the room dressed in a dark blue suit and tie, instead of the NASA coveralls with the homemade Mars mission patch he had worn to the first meeting. That had been an enthusiastic exchange of ideas, a brainstorming by some of the best minds in the business. This meeting was almost a eulogy for the mission.

Morris grabbed a nearby chair and flipped it around backwards before sitting down. "Okay," he said, "is everyone here that needs to be here?"

There were a few quiet nods of assent.

"The purpose of this meeting today is twofold, folks. First, I want your best thoughts on the possible status of the crew. Second, any ideas you may have on anything we can do to help them."

Ken Coltrin spoke up first. "Most of us believe the crew *is* alive, but for some reason they can't lift off from the Martian surface. It's probably the fuel, or maybe damage to the MEV. They've had two good launch windows between those dust storms, and they have not taken advantage of either one."

"What windows?" Morris said.

"They had twenty-four hours of clear weather after the estimated time of touchdown. Four days later, they had a ten-hour window. It's been nothing but dust storms since. If they could have fired those engines and headed back to the *Lincoln*, they would have done so already."

One of the MEP engineers in the back of the room stood up. "Now that we know they landed in the Terra Meridian, we also know they used a lot of fuel in a landing. They are probably over the curve by at least two thousand pounds or more. Every scenario we ran in the simulator shows us this."

Andy Collins, bleary-eyed from almost constant work since the Mars crew vanished, waved his hand. "This is what we know for sure," he said. "The crew followed the module to the surface. They would have burned a lot of extra fuel to land in the Terra Meridian. Images from the *Abraham Lincoln* show two separate craft making Mars entry. No fireball, no crash was seen." He paused for a moment. "Most importantly, a living, breathing human being has deployed a science package on Mars. That means at least one of the crew is alive. The seismograph signal came from the same general area as the cargo module. Put those facts together and you have a good picture of the situation." Collins walked to the front of the room and stood next to Jim Morris, who stepped aside to listen.

"The signal from the seismograph tells us more than you think," Collins continued. "If the MEV had crashed, or if some of the crew were injured or dead, no one would bother with deploying any science packages. It means all three of them are probably still alive. My team thinks the crew used too much fuel in the landing, and that they intend to transfer fuel from the cargo module. Unfortunately, the dust storms are making that impossible for them."

Ken Coltrin spoke up. "And the general terrain stinks. They couldn't have picked a worse landing site if they'd planned it."

Morris interrupted. "Is there anything realistic we can do from here to help them?"

"Nothing that we're not already doing," said Coltrin. "Not without communications. The Mars Orbiter is passing over Terra Meridian every seventy-five minutes now, but the images we're getting just show a dust storm."

"How long could the storm last?"

"No one can answer that with any certainty," said Coltrin.

"Look," said Morris, "one thing we all agree on is about the crew's chances of even *reaching* the cargo module. The beacon signal shows the module came down in either a canyon or a crater. Unless something changes, I think we should prepare for the worst."

"I think," said Coltrin, "everyone's accepted that possibility."

"Unfortunately," said Morris, "I have the unpleasant job of briefing the President on the situation. This meeting is over." As he exited the room, he slammed the door behind him, not in anger at the MEP team, but in sheer frustration.

As Morris headed back to his temporary office at JPL, he passed a few people in the hallways. Everyone he saw looked dejected. This was the most crushing blow to NASA in its entire history, perhaps even worse than the two shuttle disasters or the Apollo 1 fire. He knew that after the nation mourned their collective loss, they would not only demand answers, but the heads of those responsible, and some huge budget cuts. Morris was indifferent to the idea of the budget cuts. He only wished he could break the news to the astronauts' families in a way that would help ease their pain. On that problem, he came up empty.

He entered his office and went straight to the telephone. He used the special direct line to the President.

"Oval Office," said a professional-sounding female voice.

"This is James Morris from NASA, for the President."

"Yes, sir. The President is expecting your call. One moment please."

A few seconds later, the familiar voice of Graham Richardson came on the line. "Hello, Jim."

"Hello, Mr. President. I just finished meeting with the MEP team. I have some updates for you."

"Good," said Richardson. "I'm holding another press conference in less than an hour. I've decided to release the information about the signal from the science package. I've already spoken to the astronauts' families. Do you have anything else I should know?"

"Yes, Mr. President. We do believe the crew is still alive. That's the good news. The bad news is we don't think they can lift off from the Martian surface. They've had two good launch windows, and they haven't taken advantage of either one."

"Why not?"

"According to every program we've run in the simulator, the area where they landed is so rugged; they would have had to burn extra fuel just to locate a safe landing site. We think they simply don't have enough fuel remaining to make orbit, and the deep canyons in that area may be preventing them from reaching the stored fuel on the cargo module."

"Is there anything we can do?"

"Not really, sir. Without communications, all we can do is wait and keep searching for them with the Mars Orbiter. We've had no luck on that, because of the dust storms."

"I am truly sorry, Jim."

"Everyone is, Mr. President."

"This is not your fault. NASA only tried to do what I asked you to do. If this is anyone's fault, it's mine. I intend to take full responsibility. Is there anything you want me to say on behalf of NASA and MEP at the press conference?"

"You could ask people to pray, sir. God's the only chance those three have now."

'We're Running Out of Time'

December 21

While the cabin heater fans and air scrubbers hummed softly in the background, Johnson studied the control boards from the pilot's seat. Her dark hair was matted from the lack of a suitable bath. The fuel cells required most of their meager water supply and none could be spared for washing. She watched the oxygen numbers creep downward with each second that passed. They had less than a hundred hours remaining before the O-2 tanks ran dry.

The interior of the MEV was a complete mess. The prevailing odor was a combination of old food and unwashed bodies. Empty meal packs were strewn near the airlock door, along with assorted metal pieces stripped from the lander for disposal.

It was the middle of the Martian night again, and McKendrick and Walker were sleeping on the deck. Outside, the storm was still blowing hard. A small stone would strike the hull occasionally with a metallic ping. Each time this happened, Johnson automatically checked for any cautions-and-warnings. The MEV had endured this cruel punishment for days on end without major damage, except for the solar panels used to recharge the emergency batteries. Those had been punched full of holes by flying rocks until they died. The fuel cells were now their only remaining power source.

Sleep escaped Johnson tonight. She rubbed her forehead and yawned, and then forced herself to lay back and close her eyes. She had run scores of scenarios though the computer, trying desperately to figure out a way home. *McKendrick is right*, she thought. *We have to go to where the fuel is, and soon.*

"What was that?" McKendrick asked.

Johnson realized that she had spoken aloud, and awoke from her dozing with a start. "I was thinking out loud."

"You said something about the fuel."

"You're right. We have to move this lander to the module. We're running out of time."

McKendrick sat up and leaned against the wall. "I'd rather try that instead of sitting here waiting to die. Maybe we should fire up this bird right now."

"You can drop that idea for now," Walker said firmly. He was awake now, and sitting up on his elbows. "We can't fire the engine in this storm. Those winds would pitch us over before we got fifty meters off the ground. If the storm breaks, then we can try it."

Johnson tapped on an overhead gauge. "Wind speed is down to thirty knots. It's dropped ten knots in the last hour. Maybe it's time."

"She could be right," McKendrick said. "Maybe we should take a chance."

"Not in the dark," said Walker.

Johnson took a deep breath. "We can do it in the dark, but that's only part of the plan."

"What plan?" said Walker.

"You and Dale will have to drive the rover to the cave, walk through to the other side, and then climb down into that canyon to the module. I'll need your help from the ground, giving me lights and direction."

"You want to pilot the MEV by yourself?" said Walker.

"We need to conserve every drop of fuel we have. Not having you two on board during the transfer will save a lot of fuel. You'll have to make your way to the module on the ground." She sat up. "Just give me some lights down in that canyon and I'll put the MEV right on top of them. Trust me."

"Sounds reasonable," McKendrick said. "We can take flashlights and lay them out in a triangle. That should give you enough light."

"The wind will flip you over before you reach the top of the canyon," said Walker. "Forget it."

"You have any better ideas?" Johnson said.

"Yes. We wait for the storm to pass, and then check out the module together, before making any decision to move."

Johnson pointed to a particular gauge on the control boards. "See this? Cabin O-2. We've got less than ninety-seven hours left."

"Getting ourselves killed trying to move in high winds isn't the answer, Anna."

She checked the outside wind speed indicator. "Look. We're down to twenty-eight knots now. I say we go as soon as the wind drops enough for you two to take the rover. We've jettisoned enough weight so that if I'm the only one aboard, we might be okay on the fuel. That's assuming all of the fuel on the module is intact, and that we can make the transfer."

Walker nodded. "All right, Anna. If the wind drops below ten knots, we go."

"I'll start the checklist," said Johnson, slipping back into the pilot's couch.

A sharp burst of light flashed on the horizon, like a strobe. They all looked outside.

"What the hell was that?" said McKendrick.

The light blazed again, throwing a red-white streak across the darkness. A mountain appeared for a split-second in the distance, as more streaks crackled through the sky.

"It's lightning!" Walker exclaimed. "Did you see it?"

"It's different from lightning on Earth," said McKendrick. He squinted to see better through the scarred window. "It's very thin, and it looks red, I think."

"We get hit by any of it, we've had it," said Johnson. "Looks like it might be moving this way."

Less than an hour later, McKendrick and Walker had donned their

EVA suits and were now working outside the MEV, struggling to secure some extra equipment into the rover. Every pound they could unload from the lander and carry with them to the module was fuel saved for the transfer.

It was pitch dark, except for the strange red lightning cracking sporadically in the mountains. The wind had finally died to a soft breeze.

They finished their work and climbed into the vehicle. Walker switched on the electric motor and drove forward about ten meters to check the rover's systems. "No damage from the storm," he reported to Johnson.

"Roger that," she replied from inside the MEV.

He turned on the lights and the rover's high-intensity halogens lit up the riverbed for a hundred meters ahead. He stopped and both men turned around in their seats to watch the MEV. "Okay, Anna," Walker announced. "We're far enough away now. Go ahead and jettison."

They had agreed to try jettisoning the emergency parachutes and the metal cover securing them, in order to save weight. They would take a chance the heavy steel cover would not come crashing down on the MEV.

"Roger." Johnson flipped up a protective plastic cover and pressed a button. There was a loud bang, and then the hatch cover flew high into the air. She half-expected it to crash right back down on top of the lander. However, it fell to the ground some distance away with a clang.

Three orange-and-white parachutes settled around the lander like fluttering sheets on a clothesline.

"Nice job, Anna," called McKendrick. "It came down about twenty meters from the MEV."

"Sheer luck, guys. Clear the 'chutes and the lines and then get moving."

Walker and McKendrick walked back to the MEV, each carrying a pair of snap-cutters. They severed the thick nylon lines from all three parachutes, rolling them up neatly into coiled loops and stacking them in the rover. When they finished, they pulled the parachutes free and moved them some distance from the lander. They laid a few large rocks on top of the parachutes to prevent them from blowing around and causing a nuisance.

"That's it," said Walker over his suit radio. "The parachutes are clear. We're out of here."

"Roger that," said Johnson. "Be safe out there, guys."

As the rover bounced away up the riverbed, Johnson flashed the landing lights at them for good luck. After they disappeared around a bend, she switched off the lights to save power. She could hear them talking back and forth for some time, and then their voice signals faded into static.

The plan was simple. She would wait for a signal flare before firing the engines and moving the MEV up and over into the canyon.

She activated the video camera, pointing it slightly up and toward their destination. The picture showed only a jet-black screen and an occasional flash of lightning.

She had not trained for this maneuver. No one at NASA had thought it would ever be necessary to re-fire the main engine on the lower stage and move the entire spacecraft. The MEV was actually designed to lift off from Mars by firing the upper ascent engines, and using the descent stage as a launch platform. She would attempt to fly the entire craft a second time directly from a ground launch – something it was never designed to do.

She completed the preliminary checklist and sat back to wait for McKendrick's signal flare.

McKendrick and Walker drove up the canyon at a slow speed.

Quick, tiny bolts of red lightning snapped in the hills around them, creating a surreal light show. The lightning made very little sound, even though dozens of bolts were flashing at any given second. They could only hear a slight crackling in their helmets. The atmosphere of Mars was too thin to carry sound well.

McKendrick reached up to an overhead console and snapped a switch. "Digital recorder," he said. "No one will believe this unless they see it."

"That's for sure."

Their voices were hollow echoes in their helmets as they spoke.

"Well, you're the one who saw the module," McKendrick said. "Can we really find that cave in the dark?"

"We'll find it."

An occasional hard gust of wind pushed against their backs.

With McKendrick using a flashlight to scan the hills on their right, they rumbled up the riverbed at a speed slower than a walk. It was nearly a half-hour before McKendrick spotted the large black hole in the cliff. "There it is," he said, pointing his light at the cave entrance.

Walker shut off the motor. Going around to the rear of the rover, he retrieved a large backpack, and stuffed the parachute lines into it. He found a hammer and some sections of metal pipe the size of tent stakes. He placed them carefully into the pack, as well.

McKendrick checked to make sure he had the signal flares in his pockets, and then joined Walker at the back of the rover. He gathered all four of their flashlights and started to place them in a bag.

"Let me have three of those lights," said Walker.

"I can carry them. Hell, you're overloaded now."

"You're not coming with me. I'm going on alone."

"Why?"

"I want you to stay on this side and send up the flares from here. Johnson will never see them from the bottom of that canyon. It's too deep. There's a com system on the module. I'll let you know when to fire the flares. As soon as you do, come on through. Now give me those flashlights."

McKendrick handed them over and Walker tied two of them to the outside of his backpack with a short piece of nylon line. He carried the other in his free hand. When he finished, he started making his way up the hill.

The two men gradually picked their way up the short grade with cautiously placed steps. The terrain leveled out as they reached the mouth of the cave. Walker shined his flashlight into the cave. It was dark and ominous. He checked his oxygen. "I've got twenty-eight

142

minutes," he said. "How about you?"

"Thirty-one. We'd better hurry, Mike."

"I will. Give me seven or eight minutes to get through the cave, another five to set the rope and test it, and eight more to get back here. Got it?"

"That's cutting it pretty close. I'll bring the spare O-2 up here while you're gone. We'll switch tanks as soon as you return. Keep an eye on your time. Don't take too long."

"I won't." Walker turned and entered the cave. His flashlight was visible for a few seconds, and then he was gone.

Fall from Grace

A nna sat quietly in the pilot's seat, watching the video screen intently. It still showed only black, with an occasional flash of sparkling red from the lightning storm. She worried that she would not be able to tell the difference between the lightning and a signal flare. In the half-hour or so since Walker and McKendrick had driven away, she had climbed into her EVA suit and helmet.

She checked the digital clock and made a mental note. The two men were carrying enough oxygen for sixty minutes, and spare oxygen enough to last another sixty. They had already used a quarter of their supply. She took a deep breath and tried to stay calm.

As the minutes slowly ticked past, she became more worried. She turned the volume on the cabin radio to maximum and listened intently for a voice, any voice. She heard nothing but the frustrating sound of harsh static. She was ready to launch the MEV on a moment's notice, anticipating a go signal sometime soon.

You can do this, she thought to herself. She pulled her restraints tighter and continued staring at the video screen.

Walker made his way cautiously through the tunnel-cave. In one hand, he carried the pack with the ropes and the two extra lights.

In the other, he carried the remaining flashlight. He panned the light liberally in all directions. He noticed again how smooth and even the walls appeared. *Almost as if someone – or something – had carved it from the stone on purpose,* he thought.

The thought made him shiver involuntarily. He kept moving.

Exhaust from his air supply hissed out through a port in his helmet as he walked. It crystallized instantly and drifted to the cave floor as flakes of synthetic snow. For the first time, he noticed the floor of the cave was unnaturally smooth.

After some tremendous effort, McKendrick finally managed to haul both spare oxygen tanks up to the mouth of the cave. He laid them gently on the ground. He stared into the darkness and saw a tiny light in the distance that seemed to be moving and growing smaller. *Walker,* he thought. He checked the O-2 timer on his wrist. He had eighteen minutes before it was time to switch tanks. "Mike?"

"I hear you," came a faint reply. "What is it?"

"Better hurry. You're down to less than twenty minutes."

"Understood. I'm almost to the far side of the cave. I think I see the exit."

"Roger that." McKendrick picked up the oxygen tanks. *The hell with firing the flares from this side,* he thought. *He's running out of oxygen over there.* He headed into the cave.

Walker came to the opening and the ledge on the far side of the tunnel and immediately shined his flashlight down into the canyon. He spotted the module. "I see the MCM," he called out over his radio. There was no answer. He dumped out the pack and picked up one of the metal tubes. He pounded it into the ground with the hammer, leaving only enough sticking up to secure a rope. He hurriedly tied four of the other ropes together to make one longer one, and then tied one end of the combined rope to the spike. Tossing the rope over the edge, he watched it with his flashlight to ensure it was long enough to reach the bottom of the canyon.

The end of the rope settled about ten meters above the canyon floor. He pulled the rope back up quickly, tied on another section, and then tossed it down a second time. It reached bottom with a couple of meters to spare.

He grasped the rope firmly and tugged on it a few times. It felt strong. Easing himself over the edge of the drop, he leaned backward and pulled on the rope again.

Without warning, the spike popped free of the ground. Walker flailed his arms helplessly, the limp rope still in his hands. He tumbled backwards, crashed onto his side, and rolled headfirst into the canyon. He shouted out a curse, and then his helmet smashed into a rock, banging his head against the side. He slid down over loose rocks and gravel until he finally came to a stop at the bottom. He did not move.

McKendrick went deeper into the tunnel, searching for a light or some sign that Walker was returning. "Mike!" He saw nothing except darkness. "Mike! Answer me, damn it!"

After about fifty meters, he saw a smaller tunnel branching off to his left. He turned toward it. He saw something glowing in the distance. Even though time was short, he decided to have a quick look. He soon reached a spot where tons of rock had fallen from the ceiling and blocked the path. Pale light was leaking through small openings in the rock. He knelt down and tried to look past the rocks, but could not tell what the light was, or what was beyond it. *What the hell is that?* He thought. McKendrick began pulling some of the rocks out of the way and tossing them off behind him. Within a minute he had broken through to the other side just enough to get a good look. It was a mineral deposit, glowing green in spots along the walls. A moment later, he gasped. There was a pattern in the deposit, like symbols. *It's not a mineral deposit*, he thought, *it's some kind of pigment applied to the walls! Where have I seen those symbols before? Sweet Jesus! Somebody's been here before us!* He snapped a quick picture of the phenomenon with his helmet camera and headed back to the main tunnel.

Where are they? Johnson thought. She was keeping the descent engines powered to full warm-up, ready to fire at any moment, and she had already locked the module's position into the navi-computer for the short flight to the canyon. Keeping the MEV on warm-up mode was eating power from the ignition batteries at an alarming rate. She knew she would not be able to draw down the batteries much longer, perhaps half an hour at most.

Then she would have to either fire the engines or shut down the launch system and recharge the warm-up batteries from the fuel cells. She kept her eyes glued to the video screen and said a silent prayer for the first bit of luck since their landing – the lightning storm had finally passed. It would make it easier for her to spot the flares.

Doubt was creeping into her mind about waiting for a signal from the two men. Her female intuition began to tingle. She had a strong sense that something was already wrong.

She decided to wait another twenty minutes, and then she was going to fire the engines and find the module, with or without help from the men.

McKendrick reached the end of the long tunnel and looked down into the canyon. Even in the pitch-black darkness, he easily spotted the white hull of the cargo module. Picking up one of the flashlights that Walker had left behind; he switched it on and scanned the area below. He saw Walker lying motionless near the cargo module. The rope was scattered around his body.

"Mike!" McKendrick dumped out the larger bag with the remaining ropes and tied a few of them together. A quick examination around the lip of the drop told him what had likely happened. A small hole remained where a spike had once been planted. He grabbed three more spikes and pounded them into the ground in a tight group, to provide added strength. He secured the makeshift rope to the spike combination and lowered himself over the edge. He double-wrapped the rope around one arm, and carried the two oxygen tanks in the other. He made his way down to the canyon floor as quickly as he dared with the heavy load. A few minutes later, he finally reached the bottom and hurried over to

Walker. He knelt and shined the flashlight into the injured man's helmet.

Walker was unconscious, but breathing. Blood was sprayed around his mouth and more blood dripped from a cut on his scalp. His eyes were closed.

McKendrick rolled him over on his side to switch his oxygen tank and Walker groaned in pain. Ignoring this, McKendrick shut off the flow valve and quickly changed the tank. He followed this by doing the same with his own. After he set the near-empty tanks aside, he examined Walker a second time.

Walker's suit was still pressurized.

"Mike! Can you hear me?"

Walker's eyes fluttered open for a second, and closed.

"Mike!"

There was no response.

The caution-and-warning light caught Johnson by surprise. She turned off the annoying buzzer and reset the offending switch. It lit up a second time, followed by the master alarm buzzer, which she also disabled. This time, she did not reset the switch. The caution light had told her she could keep the MEV at warm-up for only another two minutes before it became necessary to recharge the ignition batteries.

She glanced briefly at the video screen. No flares streaked across the black Martian sky. *Why haven't they signaled?* She thought. Every fiber of her being screamed out to fire the engine right now and GO! She reached for the ignition sequence switch and then took her hand away just as quickly. *No, not yet. They still have fifty-five minutes of oxygen left and it's only a five-minute flight to the module. Patience, Anna. Wait for the signal.*

"Damn it!" She shut down the warm-up and started recharging the batteries from the fuel cells. Her frustration was reaching supreme levels.

McKendrick propped Walker up against the hull of the cargo module. He could do little for him. Walker's hair was plastered in

148

blood and he was still unconscious, but breathing steadily. From the unnatural position of the left leg, he suspected Walker's leg was broken, as well.

McKendrick pulled one of the two small emergency flares he carried from a pocket on his suit and shot it into the night sky. A bright red ball of flame streaked upward along the walls of the canyon like a Roman candle. It fizzled out and faded away before it even cleared the summit. He tried a second flare, with the same result. Although it was only about twenty meters up to the mouth of the cave, it was a hundred meters to the rim of the canyon, and far beyond the range of the emergency flare.

He walked to a reasonably flat spot about twenty meters from the module and placed a flashlight upright on the ground. He gathered a few rocks to hold it in place. The tight blue beam shone brightly into the sky. When he finished, he went back to check on Walker.

"Mike, can you hear me?"

Walker's eyes opened. He tried to touch his head, but was stopped by his helmet. He groaned and let his hand fall back to the ground. "What happened?"

"You fell. Looks like you cut your head, and I think your left leg's broken. Take it easy."

"Johnson?"

"She'll be here. Don't worry."

"How's our O-2?"

"We've got about forty-five minutes. I set up a light for her. How are you doing?"

"Not so good." Walker tried to sit up and gasped in pain. "I think you're right about my leg. It hurts like hell. I feel dizzy, too."

"You probably have a concussion. You're lucky you didn't breach your suit."

Walker made a weak effort to smile. "Yeah, right. Lucky? That would be a first for me on this mission."

"I have to agree, buddy. You look like hell."

"I *feel* like hell. Look, I want you to open the access door on this module and have a look inside," said Walker. "We need to find out if it's intact. It has an interior light system that will help Johnson see us. Go ahead. I'll be okay."

"All right." McKendrick left him sitting while he found the door leading into the module. He unlatched it and pulled it open. Small lights in the ceiling flared to life, casting a harsh white glow on everything. The module was stacked from floor to roof with sealed plastic boxes and containers of every size and description. The content of each box was clearly marked on all sides. It was all the equipment needed for a long-term visit to a hostile planet. Most of it was broken apart or crushed from the hard landing in the canyon, and useless.

There was breathing oxygen on board, but when he checked the tanks he saw they had been breached in the landing and were empty. He went to the rear of the module to check on the fuel canisters, hoping they had not suffered the same fate.

Five circular stainless steel tanks were mounted in a row against the back wall. He inspected each one carefully. They were undamaged, and all of the gauges showed the tanks were still full. Valves and high-pressure lines for pumping the fuel were secured to the same wall. He went outside and found Walker.

"Well?"

"All the fuel tanks are good," he said. "Transfer gear is still in place."

"Well, that's something," replied Walker.

"There's some bad news, though. The O-2 tanks were cracked during the landing. They're empty."

"Doesn't matter. At least the fuel is there. What about the other gear?"

"Most of it is trashed. We weren't staying here for a hundred and twenty days, I can tell you that."

"Did you check the pressure readings on those tanks? Sometimes they overfill them a bit as a sort of reserve."

"No. I just looked to see if they were intact." McKendrick knew that no matter what Walker had said, the possibility of the tanks being purposely overfilled was highly unlikely. Payload on the mission had been calculated right down to the last ounce. He glanced at his oxygen readout. They had forty minutes. He wondered if he should try to make it back to the MEV on his own and guide Johnson to the site. He decided against it. Not only would the MEV burn extra fuel dragging him along, but there was not enough time for him to get back to the MEV. He settled down next to Walker to wait. As an afterthought, he adjusted his oxygen flow down a bit, and did the same on Walker's suit. "A few extra minutes," he explained. "May as well stretch out what we have."

Walker nodded. He sat back against the module and groaned at the pain in his leg. "I saw you trying those little emergency flares. We need the larger ones."

"Where are they?"

"Guess."

"Back up there in the cave passage?"

"Right."

"I'll go up," said McKendrick. "No problem. How the hell did you end up falling, anyway?"

"I was testing the rope. I climbed over the edge and jerked on the line a couple of times. The damn spike came right out of the ground. By the way, this is the second time I've cut my head open on this mission."

McKendrick rose to his feet with an effort. "You're still alive, so I guess that means you must be hard-headed. I'm going back up for those flares now."

"Watch out for loose rock."

McKendrick found the rope and jerked on it a few times. It held firmly. He bent over slightly and began pulling himself up the steep slope. He kept a tight grip on the line and tried to place his feet on the larger rocks. He almost stumbled once, but recovered. He reached the small ledge at the mouth of the cave and crawled onto it at last. "Made it," he whispered.

Walker heard the whispered comment on his suit radio. "Good job, Dale."

"I found 'em," said McKendrick.

"Fire a couple off from up there."

"Roger that." McKendrick opened the bag and pulled out

something that looked like an oversized road flare. He pointed it skyward and jerked on a ring-and-lanyard device attached to the bottom. A bright blue-and-white rocket shot high into the Martian sky, lacing upward and over the ridge, disappearing on the far side. He fired two more in succession and watched them follow the path of the first.

By now, he was panting hard and his faceplate fogged. The exertion of climbing the ridge and firing the flares had overtaxed his air supply. He turned the oxygen flow back to full and found he could breathe again. He also saw he was down to twenty-six minutes of air. Leaning back, he fired another flare. It cleared the canyon rim easily.

Moving Day

J ohnson used a tiny joystick to operate the MEV's video camera. She scanned it slowly back and forth, zooming in the picture occasionally. She saw nothing encouraging. It was blank, except for some background light from the Martian moons. She checked the clock again. Walker and McKendrick had less than thirty minutes of oxygen.

She wiped some sweat from her forehead and uttered a soft curse. She was exhausted and depressed, as well as unwashed. She gulped down the remainder of a cup of coffee sitting nearby. It was cold.

The warm-up batteries were now fully charged. She switched on the system and waited for a green light. Johnson was torn with indecision and more than a little worried.

Launching the MEV she could do, making a bad choice she could not. She wondered if the men were already heading back on foot. If she launched, she could miss them and be unable to return in time to pick them up before they ran out of air. However, if Walker and McKendrick were waiting at the module, they could die for the same reason if she delayed too long.

The green light flashed on the engine warm-up system. She bit her lip and stared at the indicator, still undecided. She ran the possibilities through her mind, but she was tired and her brain worked slowly. The most likely scenario, she decided, was that Walker and McKendrick had reached the module without incident – and that they were waiting for her.

I have to go to them. No, she thought. *Just a few minutes more.*

At that very moment, she saw the flares clearly on the video screen. *Yes!*

She reset the master arming switch on the descent engines. This flight was to be a short hop, only ninety seconds total. She was determined to do it in less, if possible, in order to save fuel.

Johnson worked the launch checklist from memory. She hesitated for a fraction of a second at the engine-start button, and then pressed it firmly.

It fired at once with a muffled roar, sending a rush of adrenalin streaking through her body. The MEV lifted off without a hitch, shoving her deep into her seat. It gained altitude quickly, and was soon above the canyon rims and plateaus of the Terra Meridian. She checked the burn clock and worked the manual controls carefully, keeping a close eye on the navi-computer screen. The detailed radar images showed both her position, and the module's.

She leveled off the ascent and flew horizontally, following the course set by the navi-computer. In less than thirty seconds, she was already crossing over the ridge that dropped away into the canyon. All she could see were shadows. She held a hovering position for a few seconds, burning precious fuel and staring out her side window into the blackness.

Suddenly, a blue-and-white flare streaked out of the darkness from below like some alien surface-to-air missile. Nothing in her life had ever looked so beautiful.

She cut power to the engines and dropped into the canyon at once. It was about a hundred meters to the ground, and she was

154

descending at a breakneck ten meters per second.

She risked another glance out the window. *Where were the signal lights?* It was like flying into a well. She kept one hand ready on the engine throttle control, but forced herself to leave it alone for a few more seconds.

Barely forty meters above the ground, she finally caught sight of a single beam of light pointing a blazing white finger into the night. She adjusted course and brought the MEV directly over the light, and then put the spacecraft into a vertical descent.

The contact light flashed. She shut down the engine immediately. The burn clock read sixty-six seconds. She let out her breath in a long sigh and heard a friendly voice in her helmet.

"Good job," said McKendrick. "You're dead center in the spot I picked. I think the engine exhaust melted the flashlight, though. We'll have to deduct it from your paycheck. Nice work, Anna."

"Thanks. It sure is good to hear your voice. Both of you better get inside before you run those 0-2 tanks dry."

"Roger that, and we're going to need the med kit. Walker is hurt. He's going to be okay, but his leg's broken."

"Oh, Jesus. I'm on my way."

"Stay there," said McKendrick. "We'll be at the airlock door in a minute. Just get that med kit ready."

"Understood." Johnson unfastened her helmet and set it aside. She located the kit and went to the airlock just in time to see the two of them climbing through the outer door. McKendrick was helping Walker crawl across the threshold. She could see blood all over the inside of Walker's helmet. *Not again*, she thought.

McKendrick sealed the outer hatch and gave Johnson a thumbs-up. She slapped the emergency repress valve and a tone sounded when the pressure was equalized. She pulled the inner door open and climbed inside to assist the two men.

"How is he?"

"His leg's broken, all right. He cut his head against the inside of his helmet, too."

She helped him carry Walker into the main cabin. They laid him out on the deck.

Walker's leg was turned at an unnatural angle and he was again unconscious.

"How did it happen?"

"He fell."

"Let's get him out of the suit," Johnson said.

December 22

Walker was sleeping peacefully in the right-hand couch, in the fully reclined position. His broken left leg had been set and splinted. He was wrapped in a sleeping bag with the injured limb propped up on McKendrick's own rolled-up bag.

McKendrick had settled for a Mylar space blanket and the hard titanium floor to pass the night. He preferred it to the cramped confines of the couches, because of his height. Johnson lay in the pilot's couch, dozing.

Sunrise on Mars was still three hours away, so they were catching what rest they could before daylight. At first light, it would be time to go to work, transferring every drop of fuel from the nearby cargo module to the MEV. After the transfer, they would know where they stood about going home. Working in the dark had already caused one disaster, from now on they agreed to work only in daylight.

McKendrick had been the one to set Walker's leg. He had started by giving Walker a shot of morphine from the medical kit. After McKendrick asked him if he was ready, he had pulled the leg from knee and ankle and fitted the bone back into its proper place. McKendrick then attached a two-piece plastic splint to the leg, to hold it firm.

Johnson had stitched up a deep gash on Walker's scalp, and attached a dressing. Then the two of them had laid Walker on the couch to rest.

An hour before dawn, Johnson heard something familiar. She stirred in the couch, trying to ignore it. As her mind began to clear, her heart sank. She sat up on her elbows and glanced over at one of the windows.

156

McKendrick was already up and looking out the window. He shook his head in frustration. "Our old friend is back. Just our luck."

Small pebbles and sand were already beginning to pound the lander in a renewed fury, as if the planet was seeking revenge for trying to escape its clutches. The cabin lights flickered, and then the MEV was suddenly plunged into darkness.

Johnson reached up and flipped a switch on the control panels. Red emergency lights, powered by the reserve batteries, cast a strange crimson glow on their faces. "Don't worry," she said, "that was an automatic shutdown by the computer to prevent any short circuiting from the fuel cells. They don't like to be shaken around. I'll reset it later when the wind dies down."

McKendrick stared out the window. "How long do you figure it'll take the two of us to do the fuel transfer?"

"The mission plan estimates a full day, with three of us working. There's only one set of lines and valves. Each tank must be individually pumped, and very slowly. Takes time."

"Any chance we can tough it out and try it in this storm, maybe using safety lines on our EVA suits?"

"Don't even think about it. That wind is moving at over forty knots. We would puncture our suits in a dozen places before we even reached the module."

Walker slept quietly unaware, still under the heavy anesthetic of the morphine injection.

Johnson glanced at the oxygen readouts again. They had less than sixty hours remaining. She reached across the panels and lowered the partial pressure of oxygen again, as much as she dared.

Pictures

December 23

I t was the day before Christmas Eve. Children smiled at each other and their eyes widened, as each thought of trees and presents and what was hidden beneath those trees.

In groceries and supermarkets across America and Canada, women power-shopped through the crowded aisles for that very special supper. Sometimes a man accompanied the woman; however, his role was usually more supportive than contributory to the actual menu.

Harried clerks wrapped gifts and worked the checkout stands as the biggest consumer day of the year approached. The economy was good and people were spending this year.

Nevertheless, a certain atmosphere, a quiet dread, shone in the faces of people as they passed each other in the aisles. Everyone discussed it in the checkout line. Racks of magazines screamed out headlines about it. It was one of the rarest of things, an event that brought all people together, although not for something good.

This was a sad Christmas, one with an entirely new meaning.

Jim Morris awoke and sat up on the small cot, rubbing his face and stretching. He pressed a button on his watch and read the numbers he had programmed a day earlier.

49:05...49:04...

It was an approximate countdown until the Mars 1 lander ran out of oxygen.

Morris went to the sink and scrubbed his face with cold water, rubbing off the excess with a cheap white towel.

Someone knocked at the door. "Jim?"

"Come on in."

Andy Collins opened the door and stuck his head inside the small room. "Can I come in?"

"Sure."

"Thanks. How long did you sleep?" Collins closed the door.

"Five hours." Morris leaned over the sink. He was exhausted. "Anything new on their status?" He asked.

"Yes. We know that at least two of them are still alive and it looks like they're preparing for a launch."

Morris spun around in surprise. "What? How do you know?"

"Images from the Orbiter. We have pictures, Jim. They've driven the rover, jettisoned gear from the MEV, in fact, they actually moved the lander to a different location and..."

Morris pushed him aside and rushed out the door. "Come on! Let's get over to Mission Control. You can tell me the rest when we get there!"

Collins followed him out at a dead run. He was barely able to keep pace with Morris down the hallway.

Howard Tyler was already in the Mission Control Center when Collins and Morris burst through the doors. Tyler took Morris by the shoulder and pointed to the video screen. "We've got live bodies on the surface," he said, smiling.

The video screen showed a rugged area of Mars from space.

There were two tiny red dots on the screen, only a fraction of an inch apart.

"The module and the lander," Morris explained. "We tracked the lander when it moved from its original landing site."

Morris cocked his head quizzically. "What are you saying? They moved the entire lander, both stages?"

"Yes. Didn't Andy tell you about the Themis imagery?"

"Sure. But how do you know they didn't just launch the ascent stage and try to rendezvous with the *Lincoln*? I don't think we should get our hopes up. They could have crashed back into the surface."

Andy Collins left the two men and went down to speak with some of the flight controllers.

Tyler shook his head firmly. "No, Jim. They did a controlled burn and moved the MEV into the same canyon where the cargo module landed. Looks like they jettisoned a lot of their equipment before they tried it."

"It's like we thought, then. They must be low on fuel," said Morris. "They're trying to cut payload. How long will it take them to transfer the fuel from the module?"

Tyler shook his head. "That's the bad news. They are in the middle of another damn dust storm. A big one. Best estimates say it could last two or three days. It takes about a day to do the fuel transfer."

"Two or three days..." Morris thought about the countdown setting on his watch. "When did they fire the engine?"

"Four hours ago. The storm hit again not long after they moved the MEV. Hold on a second." Tyler adjusted his microphone. "EECOM," he called.

"Go."

"Give me the latest numbers on their O-2."

"Forty-four to forty-eight hours, Dr. Tyler. Give or take a couple of hours."

"Do they have any options to stretch out their supply?"

"They can lower the O-2 partial pressure. They can relax and try to conserve. If they can access the extra O-2 on the cargo module, they won't have an oxygen problem."

"Make a note, EECOM. Telemetry from the module says those tanks are empty. Stay sharp now. You should have known that already. Now give me an outside number on their oxygen usage."

"Sorry about that, Flight. Fifty, fifty-five hours, tops, if they've been conserving the whole time. After that, they would have maybe an hour or two with the residual air in the cabin. But that's the best-case scenario. I wouldn't count on it."

"Roger that." Tyler stared at the big screen and tried to keep his composure. "Wish there was *something* we could do for them," he said bitterly.

"There's nothing we can do unless we could make that storm stop," said Morris. "They are on their own, God help them."

An hour later, Morris held another impromptu press conference about the current situation with Mars 1. The reporters shouted questions at him, but the answers he was able to provide were few. He told them the known facts:

At least one or more of the astronauts was still alive.

They had moved the MEV lander to the same location as the cargo module, after dumping some excess payload.

A dust storm with winds in excess of seventy kilometers an hour was still pounding the lander, and likely preventing the astronauts from trying to refuel their vehicle.

They had roughly two days' supply of oxygen remaining on board.

There was still no communication from the spacecraft.

Anything else was guesswork and conjecture.

Morris left the pressroom and headed back to his sleeping quarters just down the hall from Flight Control. He shut the door firmly and pulled a bottle of good Irish whiskey from the desk. He poured a four-finger drink into a plastic cup and drank it down in a few seconds. The alcohol burned in his throat. He opened a small refrigerator, found some bottled water, and chased down the whiskey with it.

Christmas, he thought. *Why does it have to be on Christmas?* He lay down on the bed and tried to imagine what was happening in that lonely place, so far from home. *The three of them have to be working on a solution,* he thought, *otherwise they never would have risked moving the MEV.* This thought gave him some small comfort.

Even without direct communications, everyone at Mission Control knew the score. Something organized was going on up there in the canyons of the Terra Meridian. The astronauts were obviously inventing a completely new mission plan, and that meant there was still a chance.

If only that damn dust storm would stop, he thought.

The MEV lander sat in the little box canyon with the cargo module parked about ten meters away. The unforgiving storm wailed in protest at the human interlopers. Small pebbles and grit rattled against the lander, trying to pound their way through its pressurized hull. An occasional larger rock would bang and ricochet away in the high winds. The parachutes and lines that had once enveloped the nearby cargo module had been ripped free by the storm and were long gone.

As the dust and stone continued to fly, much of the white-and-orange paint on the lander had been sanded away and small dents now dotted the exterior. The observation window in the lander that actually faced the wind was slightly cracked, but still holding cabin pressure. A few caution-and-warning lights had flashed as minor problems arose from the incessant beating, but nothing critical had been damaged – *yet.* The craft continued to rock from side to side.

Inside, the three astronauts waited impatiently among the discarded food packs, sleeping bags, and other items. They were hoping for the storm to subside, an event that would give them at least a chance to escape. They were tired and dirty. They smelled bad. Their minds, ordinarily sharp, had been worn down by a long mission, reduced airflow in the cramped cabin, and the stresses created by a situation that promised almost certain death.

One of them was still in focus mentally.

Anna Johnson continued to work different calculations through the navi-computer, figuring weight-to-thrust ratios, fuel usage, and oxygen consumption.

Johnson checked the latest caution-and-warning light that flashed after a particularly loud strike from a flying rock. "There goes the outside video," she said. "Something must have smashed the protective cover."

"Another useless item we would have jettisoned later anyway," noted McKendrick, who was relaxing on the deck reading a book.

"Those dumb paper books are going out the airlock, too," Walker said. "Haven't you ever heard of a Kindle or an iPad?" He was also on the deck in a sleeping bag, with his leg propped up on a folded-up pressure suit. He had grown tired of the couch.

"I've got a Kindle, all right. I only brought two dead tree books along. And yes, I'll ditch them out the airlock – after I finish reading them."

"How's the leg, Mike?" Johnson asked.

"Not too bad. Hurts a bit."

"You want some morphine?"

"No. Is there any decrease in the wind speed yet?"

"It's still holding at forty knots."

"What about our O-2?"

"Ten minutes less than you asked me ten minutes ago. We can get through today and tomorrow. The tanks will run dry about two hours after daylight on Christmas morning. They would have been empty already, except I cut the partial pressure pretty quick after we first landed."

"You did good stretching out our supply like that," said Walker.

"It probably won't make any difference, Mike."

"Maybe not, but you did well. That was smart thinking."

"Thanks."

"I've been sitting here trying to figure out a way to get over to the module," said Walker.

McKendrick put down his book. "Same here. You have an idea?"

"Nothing that doesn't involve some serious risk. And I'm not going to order anyone out there into that storm to try it."

"What's your idea?"

"Sooner or later, one of us will have to try for the module, storm or no storm. If that person can get inside without having their suit punctured, they can start the hookups and connect the line to the MEV to start the transfer. It means three trips outside, though. Once to get inside the module and start the process, once to connect the line to the MEV and hurry back inside the module, and then one more exposure to get back inside here after the transfer is complete."

"That means someone will have to stay inside the module switching the line from tank to tank for at least ten or twelve hours," said Johnson. "We only have about ten hours' worth of portable O-2 left on board."

"I know."

"So, it's suicide."

"I could lower my oxygen flow and try to make it last until the fuel transfer is complete," said Walker.

Johnson shook her head. "Forget it, Mike. Your leg is broken. If anyone is going out there in that storm, I am, but not until we have to."

"No. I can do it. I could order it, even."

Johnson left her couch and knelt down next to Walker. "Is this about guilt or something? Is that why you want to hobble out there on one leg and throw your life away trying to hook up those lines? You are one stubborn son of a bitch, Walker. Why don't you just shut your mouth and leave things to me."

"I'm still mission commander. I give the orders."

Johnson's eyes flashed. "You're *not* going out there."

"Who will, then? You? We need you to pilot the MEV. Dale outweighs me by thirty pounds, which means he uses more oxygen. We don't have enough portable O-2 left to give him time to make the transfer. We only get one good shot at this, Anna." Walker turned his head and stared at the wall. "Face it. It has to be me."

"And I weigh fifty pounds less than you," said Johnson. "So I use the *least* amount of oxygen. Do me a favor. Shut the hell up."

Another caution-and-warning light flashed, along with the annoying buzzer that always accompanied it. Johnson went over to check it out.

"What is it now?" Walker asked.

"Our exterior weather sensor package just flew away," she replied, shutting off the alarm.

Walker made a wry face. "Well, as long as we have windows we don't need it anyway. We can just look outside and see the weather."

For the first time in days, Johnson laughed. "I guess you're right. Besides, that sensor array weighs a good forty pounds."

"See? Everything has a bright side. We just saved some fuel."

"The sun is going down," said McKendrick. He closed the book and settled into his bag. "The more we sleep the less oxygen we use." He shut his eyes. "I suggest both of you get some rest."

"Good idea," said Walker, wriggling carefully under his own sleeping bag.

Johnson went back to the left-hand seat and stared at the numbers on the control panels regarding fuel usage and oxygen consumption – searching for answers. When she saw no new answers were forthcoming, she closed her eyes and slept.

Cocoa Beach

Christine McKendrick had kicked the covers from her bed during the night. She was splayed out on the mattress, still dressed in yesterday's clothes. When the sun peeked its way through the bedroom shades, she raised her head and looked at the alarm clock.

It was seven o' clock in the morning.

Shit. She pulled a pillow over her head and tried to go back to sleep. Her mother-in-law was due to show up at eight to take her out for breakfast. Christine knew it wasn't really a date for a holiday breakfast. It was to be a thorough grilling performed by a worried mother-in-law – an ongoing conversation regarding possibilities, scenarios, and speculations on the fate of her son.

She did not want to face the day, and she was not hungry.

Maggie McKendrick would pump her for any new information about Dale and the crew, as she had done with her unrelenting telephone calls and emails for the past two weeks.

The last call had been the straw to break the camel's back.

"I don't know, Maggie! Nobody knows!"

"You know everyone at NASA, Christine. Surely they must have

said something."

"They think they're still alive. There's nothing else to tell. NASA has been telling the news services everything they know. If I hear anything new, I'll call you right away."

Click.

That had been the end of the last telephone call.

I have to get up, she thought. *It's Christmas Eve.*

The boys are coming for dinner. Counting Phoebe, Sara, and all the grandkids that means dinner for nine. There's no food here and I don't feel like shopping today. Suppose I will have to, though.

She thought about Dale again and her mother-in-law, who was due at the door in less than an hour. She slumped back onto the pillow. *He's your son, but he's my husband and I love him, too.*

Tears rolled down her cheeks as she sobbed quietly.

A Strange Revelation

"Merry Christmas."

"Hmm?"

"Wake up sleepyhead. It's Christmas morning."

Anna Johnson rolled over on the couch and opened her eyes. She saw McKendrick sitting against the airlock door with a book in his hand. His hair was matted and dirty, and his two-week growth of gray beard made him look older. "Merry Christmas, Dale," she mumbled, closing her eyes.

"The storm's gone."

"What?" She was awake in an instant. She sat up and glanced out the window to her left. Thick dust had gathered along the outer rim of the window, but the winds that had been pounding the lander for days had finally passed. "Oh my God...how long?"

"It stopped about ten minutes ago. One second it was blowing like hell, the next it just disappeared." He tossed aside the book into their communal pile of trash and stood up. "We're not really letting Mike go out there to do the fuel transfer, are we?"

"Of course not, Dale. I'll do it."

Walker groaned and sat up on his elbows. "What's going on?"

"Storm's passed," said McKendrick. "Merry Christmas to us."

"Thank God." Walker scooted himself upright and sat up against the wall. "I'll need help to get into the EVA suit."

"Nice try, Mike. I'm not letting you go out there with that leg," said Johnson. "I can handle the transfer."

Walker shook his head. "Look, I'll admit you're in pretty good shape, but those high-pressure lines are tricky to handle. You can't do it. We discussed this. I have to be the one."

"Not a chance," she countered. "You stay in here."

"Damn you!" Walker grabbed a nearby handrail, the only one remaining that had not been stripped and discarded to save weight. He struggled to his feet. "Remember when we practiced the fuel transfer in Huntsville? Dale and I could barely connect those lines working together! How in the hell do you figure you can do it by yourself? You don't have enough upper body strength to handle the job!"

"I can do it."

"No, you can't. Besides, I want you to start running the numbers for the launch. You'll have plenty to do. Once you go out there, you'll have to stay until the transfer is complete. The gauges must be monitored constantly for pressure fluctuations, and you have to adjust the flow valves accordingly. You can't leave them for very long, it's too dangerous. By the time the transfer is complete, we won't have time to do the checklist before we run out of air. You need to have us ready to lift off the minute the fuel is transferred."

Johnson looked at McKendrick. "What do you think?"

"I think he's right. At least about having the checklist complete when the transfer is done. How much cabin O-2 do we have left?"

She glanced at the readout. "Thirteen and a half hours. Plus the cabin residual. Maybe fifteen hours. But we lose some of that each time we use the airlock."

"That's right," said Walker. "It's going to be pretty close. Now come on, give me a hand here."

"I don't know, Mike. How much can you really do with that leg?"

"It's splinted. I'll be fine. We're wasting time."

"If something goes wrong out there, if we have to waste time and more oxygen getting you back in here, we'll blow our only chance of getting home," said Johnson.

"And I'm telling you I can do it. Think of it as redemption."

Johnson rolled her eyes and laughed. "Are you kidding? Don't give me any crap about 'redemption.' You screwed the pooch on this one. If we get out of here, it will be a miracle, and not a whole lot of thanks to you."

Walker stared at the deck. "I know."

Johnson suddenly regretted the statement she had made. "I didn't mean that, Mike." She came over to him and put a hand on his shoulder. "I'm sorry."

"What the hell," he said. "This whole mission has been a waste."

McKendrick raised a hand. "Not a total waste. At least, I don't think so."

"What do you mean?" Walker asked.

"When I was in the cave I spotted a side passage and followed it until I came to a place where a rock fall had blocked the tunnel. I cleared some of the rock out the way and I saw something strange."

Johnson looked skeptical. "What did you see?"

"Symbols," said McKendrick. "Painted on the wall in a sort of phosphorescent pigment."

"Is this a joke?" Johnson said. "You're kidding, right? You're suggesting there's life here – *intelligent life?*"

"I don't know. But the symbols look familiar somehow," McKendrick replied. "You want to take a look? I snapped a picture of it. It's on my helmet cam. Look for yourself."

"Jesus..." Walker whispered. "Symbols? Now that gives me the willies. Yeah, download it and let's take a look at it on the video screen."

Johnson retrieved McKendrick's helmet and connected a plug between it and the computer. She started the download.

"The MEP guys will have a field day with this," said Johnson. She studied the symbols in the picture. Some were unfamiliar; others were in the shape of a triangle or other known forms.

"I know what these are," said Walker quietly. "At least a few of them, anyway."

"What the hell are they then?" McKendrick said.

Walker pointed to a couple of the symbols. "I saw these in a book about the Roswell incident. I'm sure of it. They were supposedly on an I-beam in the wreckage of an alien spacecraft. You know, Roswell...1947, dead alien bodies and all that."

"Bullshit," said McKendrick. "You're full of it, Mike."

"No, I'm not kidding. I'm sure that's where I saw them."

It was quiet as a church as the three of them stared at the picture on the video screen.

Walker broke the silence. "Well, I'd say the question on whether humans are the only intelligent life around has been answered, unless you think those are a natural phenomenon. And they sure don't look natural to me."

McKendrick reached up and touched the screen reverently with the tips of his fingers. "Just for the record, if we get off this rock I don't think we should tell Houston about this until we get home."

"I agree," said Johnson. She shook her head. "I'm looking at it, but it's hard to believe it. One thing's for sure, *somebody* made that."

"No one's telling Houston anything unless we can get that fuel transferred. We'd better get moving on it," said Walker.

"Okay, Mike. You can try the fuel transfer," said Johnson. "We'll help you prep. But if you have any problems out there, I want you to come back inside right away and let me give it a shot instead, agreed?"

"Agreed."

"Let's get to work then."

McKendrick stood up and stretched, his bones cracking. "Hold up. I think we need one change to this plan."

Walker hopped on one leg over to his EVA suit hanging on the wall. He took it down. "What's that?"

"Forget that stuff about body weight and oxygen usage. Neither of you can do the transfer alone. It *has* to be me."

"We already decided," said Walker. "*I'm* going."

"Not with that broken leg." McKendrick freed one of the five remaining oxygen tanks secured near the airlock. He laid it on the deck and reached for another cylinder. "Nice of you to volunteer, though," he added, smiling.

Walker looked down at his leg and shook his head. The fight flowed out of him like a deflating balloon. He hung his suit back on the wall and sat down. "All right. Go ahead then."

McKendrick laughed "Don't sweat it, Mike. I never had any intention of letting you go out there. I just let you rattle on about it to prevent another argument between you and Anna. I've trained on doing the fuel transfer more times than both of you put together."

"I remember that," said Johnson. "You put in a lot of extra hours on that exercise. Why?"

McKendrick placed the last O-2 cylinder gently on the deck. "Because I knew the fuel transfer was the most critical thing on this mission, that's why. It was *always* about the fuel, people. Always."

An hour later, McKendrick was closing the outer airlock door behind him and walking toward the cargo module in his EVA suit. As he approached the module, he saw sand drifts from the storm thrown up against the access door. He knelt down and cleared the sand away by hand, and then pulled the door open. He pushed the first two oxygen tanks inside and rolled them off to the side.

"How are you doing, Dale?" Johnson called over the radio.

McKendrick was breathing hard. "No problem. Two tanks are inside. I'm going back for the rest. The damn things are heavy, even in Mars gravity."

"Roger that. You have ten hours on the portable tanks, but only twelve minutes left on your suit tank. Don't forget to switch it out."

"Don't worry. I will." He picked up the last three tanks from near the MEV airlock and headed back to the module. He pushed those inside as well, and climbed into the module. The automatic lights came on and he shut the door.

The cargo bay was the size of a semi-trailer. It was also a mess.

He checked his suit tank. Ten minutes remained. He shut it off and switched out for a fresh one. When he finished, he took down the thick high-pressure line from its storage place and laid it on the deck. Picking up one end, he started to connect it to the first fuel storage tank.

He stopped.

"Anna?"

"Go ahead."

"The line is too short."

There was no answer.

"Anna...did you get that? The line is too short."

"Roger that. The line is short. How short?"

"It's a ten meter line. I don't know exactly how much we're short. Maybe a couple of meters."

"Can you move the fuel tanks closer to the door? Maybe if you slide the tanks over to the door the line will reach."

"Okay. I'll check it." McKendrick went back outside and paced off the distance between the tanks and the fuel feed connector on the lander. "Looks like twelve meters or so."

"Can you move the tanks closer so the line will reach the connector?"

"I'll try. Give me a few minutes. These one-ton tanks still weigh about seven hundred and fifty pounds each in Mars gravity."

"All right. Be careful."

"Always."

McKendrick went back inside the module and retrieved the high-pressure line. Rolling it out on the ground, he took the end and connected it to the inlet valve on the lander. When he returned to the module, he saw the line now reached about a meter inside the door and stopped.

"Okay," he called. "It's just inside the module door. I think we can do it if I can get the tanks close enough to the door."

"Roger that."

He went to the back wall to study the storage tanks. They were round, with flat bottoms, about a meter in diameter each and three meters high. *No one figured we'd ever have to move them,* he thought. The task looked daunting. He tried to imagine Walker trying to move one of the tanks with a broken leg.

He freed one of the tanks from a metal restraining strap that held it firmly to the wall and then tried to slide it toward the door. It was like trying to move a statue sunk in concrete. His faceplate fogged from the exertion and he stopped pushing on the steel tank for a moment. "Anna?"

"Go ahead."

"Stand by. I can't move them without a lever. I'm going to look around here for something to use."

"Roger that. Just to let you know, you've used about thirty minutes of O-2 already."

"Understood."

"You never would have been able to do anything out there," said Johnson.

Walker stared at the floor. "Maybe so, but he will never be able to pump that fuel over in time, even if he can move the tanks."

"You don't know that."

"Takes at least ten hours to do the transfer, and he has to move those tanks one at a time. He doesn't have that much air."

"Mike, do me a favor."

"What?"

"Unless you've got something positive to say – shut the hell up."

McKendrick checked his oxygen. It would be time to switch to another tank soon. He had found a thick steel tube for gathering core samples, and used it to muscle the first fuel container close enough to reach the line. When the first tank had drained, he had levered it out the door and rolled it clear. The second of the five fuel tanks was now pumping its precious liquid into the lander. The speaker in his pressure helmet crackled to life.

"Dale?"

"Go ahead, Anna."

"I'm showing two thousand five hundred and sixty-six pounds total fuel received from that first tank. Nice job."

"Well, that's good. There was only supposed to be twenty-five hundred pounds in it. Tell Mike he was right. They did squeeze as much fuel into those tanks as they could." McKendrick checked the flow meter on the second tank. The digital readout seemed to take forever to change numbers. "Too bad it takes so long to pump it over. That first one took more than two hours."

"I know. Just do the best you can."

"Roger that." He sat down on the floor of the module and watched the digital readout on the fuel tank as it continued its slow backward march. He cut back his oxygen flow as much as he dared and tried to relax.

"How's it going?" Walker asked.

"Okay, but he's going to run out of oxygen before the last tank finishes pumping."

"Anything we can do?"

"I don't know."

Walker glanced over at the two remaining EVA suits hanging on the wall over by the airlock. "How much air is left in those suits?"

"Not a lot."

"You wouldn't need more than a few minutes of air. After he connects the last tank, he should wait as long as he can to monitor the transfer, and then come back here. You can get into your suit after the fuel is transferred and go out and disconnect the inlet line. You should have enough air left to do it. Then we can get the hell out of here."

Her eyes widened. "Smart idea."

"Yeah, I'm still good for something."

"Shut up, Walker." She smiled.

"What about the outer airlock door? Don't we need to unbolt it? You wanted to leave it on the ground, right?"

"No," said Johnson. "I forgot something. It won't work. We'll expose ourselves to vacuum when Dale comes back inside."

"Not if we can get it closed without having it fall off. Tell him to remove the bolts and hinges before he comes back inside, and then close it very carefully. He should pull it tight, but not actually latch it. It should drop right off when we fire the engines. You'd better

174

move all this garbage into the passageway, too and have him toss it out before he works on the door. You'll have to leave the laser cutter out there for him, too."

"Sounds reasonable."

"I have another idea."

"What?"

"Cut off the metal bases on these two other couches and toss the couches outside, too. That will save a lot of weight."

"And what will you and Dale do? I can't have you just bouncing off the damn walls."

"We can lie on the deck. You'll have to cut some holes in the deck and string something through them to hold us down."

"You're joking."

"No. Those couches weigh almost a hundred pounds each. We'll be all right. Think you can handle the MEV solo?"

"I think so."

Walker smiled. "I guess we're going to find out."

The hours passed and the oxygen supply remaining in the lander continued to drop, while the fuel level continued to rise.

As Walker coached her, Johnson used the laser cutter to free the two couches from their mountings. She dragged them one at a time to the airlock and shoved them into the passageway. After that, she tossed in the empty food containers, the remaining food packs, and anything else she could find. Finally, she cut four small holes in the deck and looped some extra line though them by climbing down into the descent stage below the deck.

She sat down in the one remaining couch. Sweat poured down her face. "I'm tired," she said.

"Forget that," said Walker. "You've got more work to do. Start the checklist, and don't forget to program the navi-computer with the Lincoln's current orbital position. We can't lift off until we know we can catch it as it's passing over us."

"I know what to do, Mike!"

"Hey, I'm just trying to help."

She wiped her face. "Sorry."

"No problem. Better see how Dale is doing."

"Sure." She called McKendrick. "Dale?"

"I hear you."

"How goes it?"

"Last tank is in place. Pumping now."

"How much oxygen do you have left?"

"Not enough. Less than thirty minutes. Sorry. It takes a while to move the empty tanks out of the way and hook up the next one. I thought I could do it faster."

"Don't worry about it. We'll risk not monitoring the flow on the last one. I want you to get back here."

"What's the problem?"

"No problem. I need you to come back and unload everything I placed into the airlock. The laser cutter is in there, too. Then cut the hinge pins and the sealing latch from the outer door and close it carefully. I left a small piece of line for you. Tie off the door to the railing. If you don't cause the door to fall off the hinges, it should hold seal long enough for you to get back through the inner airlock. After we lift off, the pressure on the door will snap the line free and the door should drop away."

"Fine," he replied, "but who is going to disconnect the hose when it finishes pumping over the last of the fuel?"

"I will," said Johnson. "I'm getting into my suit now. How much long before the pumping is complete?"

"About fifty minutes. You have enough suit air left to move around out here and disconnect the hose?"

"There's enough. Get back here now."

"On my way."

McKendrick checked the flow meter on the final fuel tank and was satisfied. It was running normally. He stepped carefully from the module and walked back to the MEV. Opening the outer airlock, he was surprised to see two couches thrown into the passageway along with the other items.

"Anna?"

"Yes?"

"What the hell are the flight couches doing out here?"

"I'll explain later. Get rid of them and everything else in there. Don't forget to cut those hinge pins and the latch and remove them, too. You'll have to be careful closing the door afterward."

"Roger that. And then tie off the door with the line, right? I sure hope this works." He climbed inside the passageway with some difficulty, and then started tossing everything out the door.

Jim Morris, Howard Tyler, and the MEP supervisory team were right back where they started. They had assembled in a room near the Mission Control room to brainstorm the status of Mars 1.

The mood was somber and the participants exhausted. Tyler stood alone at the front. Jim Morris was dressed in a soiled white shirt and wrinkled slacks.

"All right, everyone. Listen up," said Tyler. "Our figures say the astronauts could be dead by now. However, our latest image from the Orbiter tells another story. I wanted you to see it. Jim?"

Morris used a remote to dim the lights and flash the picture of Mars 1 onto a screen at the front. The high-resolution photograph showed two tiny spacecraft on the floor of a canyon. "This was taken just thirty minutes ago," said Morris. "I'll blow it up a bit."

As everyone watched, the spacecraft grew larger until more details appeared. A black line in the photo seemed to connect the two craft.

"The black line...what is it?" Someone said.

From the back of the room, a familiar young voice spoke. "It's the fuel transfer line from the cargo module," said Andy Collins. "They're pumping over fuel from the module."

The room erupted in loud voices. Everyone seemed to leap up simultaneously and shout questions.

"Quiet down!" Tyler yelled. "All we know is that they were alive as of a half hour ago. That's it. In any event, I want everyone to return to their stations and prepare for a possible launch from the surface and a rendezvous with the *Lincoln*."

13th Day

J
ohnson kept her eye on the window at the airlock passageway. She watched as McKendrick used the laser to cut through the hinges on the outer door. Every scrap of material inside the passageway, including the two couches, had been cleared away and discarded.

Exactly forty-one minutes remained before the *Abraham Lincoln* would be in position for a rendezvous as it passed overhead. If they missed it, there was no second chance. They would be out of oxygen before it came around on the next orbit.

Johnson glanced back at the clock. It was 11:30 PM, local Mars time. She looked at Walker, who was already wrapped in a sleeping bag and secured to the deck with a few crude lines. "You look like a turkey at Thanksgiving," she said. "Or maybe that guy in *Gulliver's Travels*. Only thing missing are the little people."

"I'm sure I do. What's Dale doing out there?"

"Everything's jettisoned. He's working on the door now."

"Have him check his air."

"Dale?" She called on the radio.

"Go ahead."

"Are you about finished?"

"Give me one more minute. I'm almost there."

"Mike says check your air."

"Six minutes. No problem. I'm kind of busy here, Anna."

"Roger. Move it along, though."

"Got it."

She examined the helmet in her hands, checking the seals. "I'm going out after he comes in."

Walker gave her a thumbs-up. "Good luck."

McKendrick appeared at the inner door and tapped on the glass.

Johnson saw that he had shut the outer door and locked it, even with the hinge pins removed. She checked the airlock for proper sealing, and when she was satisfied, she flooded the compartment with air and opened the door.

McKendrick stepped inside and immediately fell to his knees, practically ripping off his helmet. He gasped and put his hands on the floor. "Jesus, that was close. My air ran out in the passage...oh, man."

Johnson put on her helmet and latched the ring seal. She turned on her oxygen and stepped into the airlock. When she reached the door, she untied the line gently and opened the door just enough squeeze her suited frame past it. She did this one careful inch at a time, so that the door did not fall off the hinge frame.

She left it open and trudged over the sand and rock to the module. Going to the back of the module, she checked the last tank of fuel. It read three hundred pounds remaining. She did a quick mental calculation. It would take four more minutes to transfer the fuel.

Dale did good, she thought. "Dale," she called. "You on com yet?"

"Go ahead, Anna."

"Four minutes left on the transfer. I'm going over to the MEV to uncouple the line."

"Roger that. I'll let you know when we get it all. Remember, close the valve first, before you uncouple the line, otherwise all the fuel in our tanks will escape into the atmosphere."

"Right. Close the valve first." She followed the fuel line over to the lander and found the coupling. "All right. I'm at the coupler."

"Okay. It won't be long."

She took the opportunity to study the connection. It was a simple device, a stainless steel handle and a round pipe.

"That's it," said McKendrick. "That's all of the fuel in tank five. Go ahead and uncouple."

"Roger." She grasped the metal valve on the outside of the spacecraft with both hands and pulled it as hard as she could. It was frozen solid. "Damn it! The shutoff valve's not moving!"

"Are you pulling on it?"

"Yes."

"Push it instead."

She braced her feet and pushed the valve handle firmly. It gave so easily that she stumbled and banged her helmet into a landing leg on the MEV. "It's closed," she said ruefully.

"We heard a loud noise in here, Anna. Are you okay?"

"Yes. Disconnecting the hose now." She spun the ring connector and the line practically popped from her hand to the ground, releasing a spurt of white vapor. "Line is disconnected," she said. "I'm coming back inside."

"Roger."

Johnson squeezed back through the airlock and cautiously closed the outer door an inch at a time, trying not to throw it off-balance and let it fall from its hinges. She examined it around the edges, trying to see if it was really closed. When she was satisfied, she re-tied the line between the door handle and the airlock hand railing. "Okay, Dale. We're good. I want you to repress the airlock nice and slow. Don't build up the pressure in here too suddenly or it could force the door open. Then open the inner hatch."

Instead of loud rush of air, Johnson waited patiently as McKendrick took his time pressurizing the airlock. She kept an eye on the door, but it did not move.

"Pressure stabilized. I don't know for how long," said McKendrick. "Let's get you in here quick."

"Roger."

McKendrick opened the inner door and helped her inside the

spacecraft. "Good job," he said.

Johnson closed the hatch with finality and pulled off her helmet. Both men were staring at her intently. For the first time, she saw something in their eyes she had never seen previously.

Trust.

"Two minutes," said Johnson. Her emotions raced; trying to substitute their own powerful forces for the calm she needed now. She held a printed copy of the launch checklist in one hand and worked the controls with her other hand from the one remaining couch. There could be no mistakes.

Walker and McKendrick were now observers, secured tightly to the deck of the MEV for a flight that was far beyond any textbook or contingency plan. No one had ever practiced for this, or programmed it into a simulator for an astronaut to solve. It was brand-new territory.

McKendrick was exhausted. He lay on the deck staring at the ceiling. He thought about his family, but in the back of his mind, he was still working. As Johnson announced the steps on the launch checklist and implemented each setting on the controls, he was ready to interrupt her if she skipped something. He had memorized the list long ago.

Walker grimaced and tried to get comfortable. The pain in his leg was intense. He thought about the g-forces that would be generated during a climb to Mars orbit, and he knew that leg was going to hurt like hell.

"One minute to ignition," Johnson announced. "We're going manual on the launch, guys. I may have to adjust trim in order to break that line loose and dump the outer door."

"Sounds dangerous," said McKendrick.

Johnson did not reply. She flipped a switch at the far end of the controls, leaning over to reach it. "Master arm switch on. Descent stage platform release on."

"Are you sure the *Lincoln* is in orbital position for us to make rendezvous?" Walker said.

"I ran the numbers three times, Mike. We should run right into it. And we still have radar, you know."

She grasped a joystick that used small rockets to control pitch, yaw and roll on the spacecraft. "Forty seconds to ignition."

McKendrick groaned. "Just for the record, I really hate being hog-tied to the deck like this."

"You two are a couple of old ladies," Johnson said. "Quit whining. Thirty seconds."

"In case we don't survive this," said Walker, "I want to apologize for what I did on the desert exercise."

"What did you do?" asked McKendrick, turning his head.

"He mixed extra salt tablets into my water bottles," said Johnson.

"You're joking."

"And he had extra water and food in his own pack," she added.

"Jesus, Mike. What the hell did you do that for?"

"I'm sorry. It was a stupid thing to do."

"Yes it was. Apology accepted," said Johnson. "Now forget it, will you? Ten seconds."

At that precise moment, the cabin fans stopped humming and came to a stop.

"We just ran out of oxygen," said Johnson.

The engines fired, spitting fire across the landscape. The top half of the lander freed itself from the spider-legged platform below and rose into the sky, slowly at first, and then much faster. The roar was deafening.

Johnson angled their ascent toward the airlock side of the lander, and was pleased to see a light blink on the controls. "There goes the outer door!" She shouted over the noise of the engines. She felt the extra lift as the heavy steel hatch dropped free and tumbled back toward the Martian surface.

Suddenly, the MEV pitched hard in the other direction, and as she had predicted, the atmosphere rushing into the airlock passage was throwing them back and forth. "Damn it!" Johnson worked the joystick control, fighting to bring the MEV back on an even keel. She grunted loudly. "Oh no, you don't..." she said to herself.

"We're pitching over!" McKendrick shouted. "Come on! Watch those gimbals!"

She ignored him and fought the g-forces that were building and pushing her into the seat. She struggled to level out the spacecraft. The ascent engines screamed as they pushed the MEV higher, but at the same time, it was angling over onto its side.

If it pitched over too far, the lander would head back toward the surface, with no hope of recovery. She managed to keep them at a safe angle – meaning the engines were pointed toward the ground – but just barely. As the atmosphere grew thinner, the shuddering finally stopped. She regained full control of the MEV. "I've got it! Hang on!"

She took a quick glance out the left window and watched the Martian surface falling away at a fast clip. "Ten thousand meters," she said.

"Damn, my leg hurts," Walker said. "How much time until rendezvous point?"

"We should have visual in about twelve minutes." She watched their fuel consumption and saw it was within limits – barely. The air inside the small cabin was already growing hot and stale. The engines burned furiously as the MEV continued to accelerate. The color of the sky changed from a light orange to black as they left the planet behind and reached a low orbit. The stars began to appear.

A small blip flashed on the radar screen. "I've got the *Lincoln* on radar," said Johnson. "Switching over to auto-guidance mode."

The computer took control of the lander and adjusted their course slightly to intercept the *Lincoln* in orbit.

A few minutes later, the lander approached the nose of the *Abraham Lincoln* and drifted toward the docking collar.

"Ten meters at one meter," said Johnson.

The tiny spacecraft bumped into the massive one and the two vehicles snapped together with a loud thump.

"Hard dock," said Johnson. She hung her head, totally spent.

"Thank God," said McKendrick.

They were going home at last.

Papers, pencils, and shouts flew around the room at Mission Control. Jim Morris and Howard Tyler hugged, both men sobbing in relief. Andy Collins had a grin that stretched from ear-to-ear, and was busy hugging every technician working the terminals.

Within two minutes, the press was informed: The astronauts were alive, back aboard the *Lincoln*, and preparing to set course for home. The news flashed around the world and people began to celebrate. It was December 25 and what had been the most depressing Christmas in recent memory had become an overwhelming triumph.

Tyler first called the families of the astronauts, and then the President – in that order. A copy of the first transmission received from Mars 1 was released to the press:

"Houston...Mars 1. We have made a successful liftoff from a canyon in the Terra Meridian and have rendezvoused with the Abraham Lincoln. We are all safe and well, and all systems aboard the Lincoln are go. Houston, please send our SRB burn data. We'd like to come home now."

"The 13th day of Christmas," said Walker from his bunk. He now wore a cast on his broken leg.

"What?" Johnson secured him to the bed with the special strap provided.

"It's midnight in Florida now. December twenty-sixth. That makes it the thirteenth day of Christmas. The day we made it off the big rock back there."

Johnson smiled and shook her head. "Wrong again, Mike. Christmas Day is the *first* day of Christmas. January sixth would be the thirteenth day, the day after Epiphany."

"Are you sure?"

"I'm Catholic. Of course I'm sure." She turned to go. "Time to jettison the MEV. You should be okay here during the SRB burn."

"Too bad we couldn't bring any samples home with us. That

184

really bothers me."

"You never get anything right, Mike." She softened the remark with another smile. "We never dumped the contingency collector. I guess I just forgot. There's forty-six pounds of Mars inside it."

As she left the cabin and closed the door, Walker's mouth dropped open in disbelief.

Resolution

Mission Day 285

Four months later, the Earth Return Capsule separated from the *Abraham Lincoln* and screamed into the atmosphere at seventeen thousand miles an hour, leaving a fiery trail that streaked across the sky. It splashed down off the Florida coast without incident, carrying three exhausted astronauts and one large container of rock and soil from the Red Planet. It was almost an anticlimax, considering the struggles the crew had endured during the mission.

Michael Walker retired from NASA within a few months. For the remainder of his life, he was hounded by people who either hated him or wanted interviews with the official First Man on Mars. Although he spoke to Anna Johnson on the telephone a few times over the years, he never saw her in person again.

Dale McKendrick joined the MEP team at the Jet Propulsion Laboratory as an advisor, and was often the keynote speaker at different NASA functions or fund-raisers. He became the real public face of the Mars 1 mission. He established a website and answered much of his email personally, especially the messages from children.

Anna Johnson returned to the Canadian Space Agency and resumed her job as Chief Astronaut. She was given practically every award it was possible to receive from both the United States and Canada. She thanked the givers for each one and they all found a place in her office. She didn't rule out the possibility of going into space in the future, but neither did she push for the opportunity. As it happened, the Mars 1 mission was the last time she ever did.

Andy Collins, the man who brainstormed the basic mission plan for Mars 1, continued to work at JPL and wrote a book about his experiences.

Graham Richardson won a second term as President. The successful return of the Mars 1 crew only served to justify his original idea to try for the Red Planet. Plans were made for a second mission, with much less time pressure on NASA and a bigger budget.

Howard Tyler retired to Southern California and bought a sailboat and a house in San Diego close to the marina.

Jim Morris took over as NASA's administrator, and eventually led the agency to even greater successes.

McKendrick's picture of the symbols on the wall of the cave were kept secret from the public. Although no one was able to decipher the symbols, the next crew to Mars were duly informed about them – and warned that they were not the only intelligent life that Mars had ever known. There were obviously many secrets about the Red Planet and it would take years to discover the truth about all of them.

Along the way, the psychological profile that NASA used to determine suitability for long-term space flight was modified, and the importance of always following the official mission plan was highly stressed to new astronauts.

The End

About the Author

Mr. Blevins camping in the Olympic mountains of Washington State in 2009

Robert Blevins is from Washington State, U.S.A. and the author of several works including, *Say Goodbye to the Sun*, *The Corona Incident*, and the crime book *Revenge Story*. His latest release is the controversial *Into the Blast – The True Story of D.B. Coope*r, written with Skipp Porteous, the founder of Sherlock Investigations in New York City. The book names former U.S. Army paratrooper and airline employee Kenny Christiansen as the famous skyjacker who jumped from a Boeing 727 with $200,000 and was never seen again. *Into the Blast* was the subject of an episode on the History Channel program *Brad Meltzer's Decoded*.

When he is not writing or editing, Mr. Blevins enjoys hiking and fishing around the Great Northwest.

You may contact the author through the Adventure Books of Seattle website at www.adventurebooksofseattle.com

www.ingramcontent.com/pod-product-compliance
Lightning Source LLC
Chambersburg PA
CBHW022109170626
46808CB00002B/661